THE END

In another minute he would be dead. A desperate measure was called for.

Suddenly taking his right hand from the lance, Fargo streaked it to his holster. He tried to hold the lance at bay with one hand, but it felt as if his throat was being crushed. Frantic, he groped for his Colt.

It wasn't there.

It had fallen out, probably when he was tripped.

Fargo's lungs were on the verge of collapse. His head was swimming. The Ute's painted features kept blinking in and out. He had only moments to live, moments to think of something to save himself.

The Ute reared to bring more of his weight to bear on the lance and yipped in triumph.

Fargo's life was fading. . . .

THE
TRAILSMAN
#366

MOUNTAINS
OF NO
RETURN

by

Jon Sharpe

A SIGNET BOOK

SIGNET
Published by New American Library, a division of
Penguin Group (USA) Inc., 375 Hudson Street,
New York, New York 10014, USA
Penguin Group (Canada), 90 Eglinton Avenue East, Suite 700, Toronto,
Ontario M4P 2Y3, Canada (a division of Pearson Penguin Canada Inc.)
Penguin Books Ltd., 80 Strand, London WC2R 0RL, England
Penguin Ireland, 25 St. Stephen's Green, Dublin 2,
Ireland (a division of Penguin Books Ltd.)
Penguin Group (Australia), 250 Camberwell Road, Camberwell, Victoria 3124,
Australia (a division of Pearson Australia Group Pty. Ltd.)
Penguin Books India Pvt. Ltd., 11 Community Centre, Panchsheel Park,
New Delhi - 110 017, India
Penguin Group (NZ), 67 Apollo Drive, Rosedale, Auckland 0632,
New Zealand (a division of Pearson New Zealand Ltd.)
Penguin Books (South Africa) (Pty.) Ltd., 24 Sturdee Avenue,
Rosebank, Johannesburg 2196, South Africa

Penguin Books Ltd., Registered Offices:
80 Strand, London WC2R 0RL, England

First published by Signet, an imprint of New American Library,
a division of Penguin Group (USA) Inc.

First Printing, April 2012
10 9 8 7 6 5 4 3 2 1

The first chapter of this book previously appeared in *High Country Greed*, the three
hundred sixty-fifth volume in this series.

Copyright © Penguin Group (USA) Inc., 2012
All rights reserved

Ⓢ REGISTERED TRADEMARK—MARCA REGISTRADA

Printed in the United States of America

PUBLISHER'S NOTE
This is a work of fiction. Names, characters, places, and incidents either are the
product of the author's imagination or are used fictitiously, and any resemblance to
actual persons, living or dead, business establishments, events, or locales is entirely
coincidental.
    The publisher does not have any control over and does not assume any responsibil-
ity for author or third-party Web sites or their content. ,

The Trailsman

Beginnings . . . they bend the tree and they mark the man. Skye Fargo was born when he was eighteen. Terror was his midwife, vengeance his first cry. Killing spawned Skye Fargo, ruthless, cold-blooded murder. Out of the acrid smoke of gunpowder still hanging in the air, he rose, cried out a promise never forgotten.

The Trailsman they began to call him all across the West: searcher, scout, hunter, the man who could see where others only looked, his skills for hire but not his soul, the man who lived each day to the fullest, yet trailed each tomorrow. Skye Fargo, the Trailsman, the seeker who could take the wildness of a land and the wanting of a woman and make them his own.

*The Mountains of No Return, 1861—
where death lurks around
every bend in the trail.*

1

"We have to be careful how we go about this. It could turn violent," Lieutenant Charles Rabitoy warned as they drew rein on a rise overlooking the lights of Hadleyville.

Skye Fargo grunted. He wasn't happy about being there. He'd signed on to do some scouting for the army, not to round up deserters.

"Something the matter?" Lieutenant Rabitoy asked.

"Don't mind him," said the third member of their party. "He hasn't had any whiskey today and that tends to make him grumpy."

"Go to hell," Fargo said.

California Jim laughed. Like Fargo, he was dressed in buckskins. Only where Fargo's were plain and well-worn, Jim's were covered with red and blue beads and had whangs half a foot long. Jim's hat wasn't plain like Fargo's, either. It was broad and high with a curl to the brim. A wide belt adorned with silver conchos was around his waist and his holster had silver studs. His bandanna, in contrast to Fargo's plain red one, was bright blue and hung halfway to his waist.

"Now, now," Lieutenant Rabitoy said. "I expect you two to get along."

"Jackass," Fargo said.

"What did you just call me?"

California Jim laughed louder. "Pay him no mind, Lieutenant. Skye and me go back a long way. We're the best of pards."

"It doesn't sound like you are to me," Rabitoy said. "And I don't appreciate his slur."

"It's just his style," California Jim said. "Ain't that right, pard?"

"You're a fine one to talk about style," Fargo said. "What was it the newspapers called you that time?" He pretended to be trying to remember, and snapped his fingers. "Now I recollect what it was." He grinned. "The prettiest scout on the whole frontier."

"Here now," California Jim said. "The scribbler who wrote that was a hack."

"Have you looked in a mirror lately?" Fargo asked.

California Jim made a sound reminiscent of a chicken being strangled. "You can go to hell, too."

"And you two are pards?" Lieutenant Rabitoy said. "Half the time, I get the impression you're ready to shoot each other."

"Shoot Skye?" California Jim said. "Why, I'd rather dig out one of my eyes with my bowie. And the same is true for him."

"Speak for yourself," Fargo said.

Lieutenant Rabitoy shifted in his saddle. "What *are* you so testy about?"

"You," Fargo said.

The young officer sat straighter. "Me? What on earth did I do?"

"You were born," Fargo said.

The pale light of the half-moon revealed Rabitoy's scowl. "I swear. I don't know why the colonel thinks so highly of you. You're impossible to get along with."

"He's not insulting you, Lieutenant," California Jim said. "He's concerned, is all, that you're so—"

"I don't need a translator," Fargo told him, and Jim fell quiet. To Rabitoy he said, "You're green as grass. You've been at Fort Barker, what, two months?"

"What does that have to do with anything?" Rabitoy said. "I was top in my class at the academy."

"Green as grass," Fargo said again. "Colonel Williams had no business ordering you to bring these men in. You're liable to get yourself killed."

"I'm perfectly competent, I'll have you know," Lieutenant Rabitoy bristled. "Besides, there are only four of them and three of us, and you two are supposed to be cocks of the walk." He said that last part sarcastically.

Fargo sighed. California had been right. He was grumpy, but only because he had a feeling in his gut that things weren't going to go well. The deserters they were after weren't about to go back quietly. Their leader was a man called Mace who had been in and out of the stockade more times than Fargo had fingers and thumbs. Mace was a bully with an especially mean streak, and had no respect for authority. "You do know that Luther Mace won't go quietly?"

"He will or else," Lieutenant Rabitoy sniffed. "I'm quite capable of taking care of myself."

"You think you are," Fargo said.

"Enough dallying," Rabitoy said. "Let's get this over with." He gigged his mount.

Fargo followed, and within moments California was beside him.

"You're being kind of hard on the boy, aren't you, pard?"

"Not anywhere near as hard as Luther Mace will be," Fargo predicted.

"That's why the colonel sent us along. To see it doesn't come to that."

"We can only do so much."

"Brighten up, will you?" California said. "Mace and those others have no idea we're after them. We'll get the drop, tie them good and tight, and take them back to the fort, as slick as you please."

"You're not just a little bit worried?"

"Not in the least."

"Liar," Fargo said.

California Jim chuckled.

Fargo didn't find it the least little bit amusing. The men with Mace hadn't enlisted to serve their country. Two were forced to join the army when they got in trouble with the law. The last was a drunk who wouldn't stop sucking down the bug juice no matter how many times he was reprimanded.

Fargo looked up. The lights of Hadleyville were less than a quarter of a mile away. He'd been there before. Like many frontier towns, it had more saloons than churches. It also had no law to speak of; the last marshal was run out on a rail.

"Let me handle this, gentlemen," Lieutenant Rabitoy remarked as they neared the outskirts and slowed. "I'm their superior."

"We have your back," California Jim said.

Fargo would rather have a bottle. He had only a few days left on his latest scouting stint, and then he'd make up for lost time.

Main Street was a riot of sights and sounds. Every hitch rail was full. Townsmen mingled with off-duty soldiers and cowboys from the nearby ranches.

There were also a handful of Chinese workers from the railroad spur. The Chinese made up a third of the population but they knew better than to roam at night. The Anti-Chinese League, as they called themselves, had already lynched two workers for no crime other than being Chinese.

"This place sure is lively," Lieutenant Rabitoy said.

"Lively as hell," Fargo dryly agreed.

The saloons were doing booming business. Liquor was only part of the attraction. There was gambling, with poker and faro and roulette, and there was the flesh trade, with more soiled doves than Saint Louis.

It was Fargo's kind of town.

"Most of the troopers go to the Bella Donna," California Jim mentioned. "That's where we should stop first."

"Surely Private Mace wouldn't be so obvious," Lieutenant Rabitoy said.

"I doubt he cares much one way or the other," California Jim said. "He's not afraid of being caught."

"That's preposterous. He has to know there are consequences to his rash act."

"Seems to me, youngster," California Jim said, "that you have the habit of assuming other folks think the same as you do."

"Well, don't they?"

"Lordy," California Jim breathed.

"What?"

Probably to be polite, California Jim didn't answer.

Fargo had no such compunctions. "The worst mistake you can make is to put your head on someone else's shoulders."

"I'd never be so foolish," Lieutenant Rabitoy declared.

"But you just—" California Jim began, and got no further.

A gunshot crashed and a man in the clothes of a backwoodsman or farmer backed through the batwings of the nearest whiskey mill. In his right hand was a smoking Smith & Wesson. He kept it trained on the saloon as he sidled to a hitch rail, bellowing, "I'll shoot the first son of a bitch who pokes his head out! Just see if I don't!"

"What's this?" Lieutenant Rabitoy said, drawing rein.

"None of our affair," California Jim told him.

A silhouette appeared in the doorway and the man with the pistol fired. He must have missed because there was no outcry. Spinning, he hurriedly reached for the saddle horn to pull himself up.

The figure came through the batwings, panther-quick, and immediately glided to one side so his back was to the wall. He wore a frock coat and a wide-brimmed black hat and had a Colt in each hand. He fired as the man by the horse spun, fired as the man's legs buckled, fired a final time as the man pitched to his knees and keeled over.

"That will teach you," the shooter said.

Lieutenant Rabitoy reined over. "Hold on there. What's the meaning of this?"

"Who the hell is asking?" the man in the frock coat demanded, coming out into the street. "Oh. A blue belly."

"I'm an officer in the United States Army, I'll have you know," Lieutenant Rabitoy angrily declared. "And I demand an answer."

"Do you, now?"

"Don't trifle with me, sir," Rabitoy warned.

The man in the frock coat still held his Colts but he didn't point them at Rabitoy. Instead, he said, "In case no one told you, pup, the army doesn't meddle in civilian matters."

"Who are you that you presume to tell me how to conduct my business?"

"Coltraine," the man said. "Jonathan Coltraine."

"Oh, hell," California Jim said.

Lieutenant Rabitoy turned in his saddle. "Do you know this man?"

"I've heard of him," California Jim said. "He makes his living at cards."

"He's a gambler?" the lieutenant said, and shook his head. "His name isn't familiar."

"He was involved in that shooting fracas down to Oro City a while back. He shot three hombres dead and wounded a fourth. Something to do with a woman."

"One of them accused me of sleeping with his wife," Coltraine said.

"Did you?" Lieutenant Rabitoy asked.

"A gentleman never tattles."

Rabitoy colored with resentment. "Your dalliances are irrelevant. It's what you just did before our very eyes that counts. And while you're right in that the army usually doesn't meddle in civilian affairs, you just committed murder on a public street. I'm taking you into custody and turning you over to the federal marshal."

"Like hell you are," Coltraine said. "I'd like to see one of you try."

Fargo had listened to enough. He reined his Ovaro past Rabitoy and said, "How about me?"

2

The man called Coltraine grinned. "As I live and breathe," he declared. "Is it really you, you ornery son of a bitch? And playing nursemaid, no less."

"Doing what?" Lieutenant Rabitoy said indignantly.

Fargo alighted and held out his hand. "It's been a spell, Jon."

The gambler holstered his right Colt and shook. "We should have a drink and catch up."

"Hold on," Lieutenant Rabitoy said. "You're personally acquainted with this man?"

"We met a few years ago," Fargo revealed. Over a card game. They'd had a lot in common and struck up a friendship.

"What happened?" he asked, nodding at the recently deceased.

"I caught him cheating," Coltraine said as he commenced to reload. "He started throwing lead. Everyone hit the floor and I came after him."

"You're saying he provoked you?" Lieutenant Rabitoy said.

"What would you call being shot at?" Coltraine rejoined.

By now others were filing out of the saloon. Some moved to the body. Others huddled and whispered and regarded the gambler warily. Coltraine ignored them.

Down the street, heads were poking out of other saloons and buildings.

"Damn," California Jim said. "This is the last thing we needed."

"What?" Rabitoy said.

"Drawing attention to ourselves."

Fargo agreed. The deserters might spot them and light a shuck. He turned to the gambler. "You wouldn't happen to have seen any sign of a soldier by the name of Luther Mace, would you?"

"Can't say as I know the gent." Coltraine finished reloading the first Colt and began on the other.

"Mr. Fargo," Lieutenant Rabitoy said, "confiscate his revolvers and we'll take him into custody."

Coltraine stopped and glanced up. "How dumb are you, boy?"

"I beg your pardon?"

"The only way you'll get these pistols is over my dead body."

People were converging from up and down the street. More than a few were soldiers.

"Mr. Fargo?" Rabitoy said again. "What are you waiting for?"

"Hell to freeze over," Fargo said.

"That was a direct order."

"You can't arrest a man for defending himself."

"Who said anything about arresting? We're merely turning him over to the civilian authorities so we can be on about our business of finding the deserters."

Fargo noticed an approaching trooper give a start. The man backpedaled, pushing others out of his way. "There's one now," he said, and pointed.

"What?" Rabitoy shifted in his saddle. "Where?"

Metal glinted, and someone hollered, "Look out! He's drawin' a gun!"

Fargo sprang and seized Rabitoy's leg. Before the officer could guess his intention, he upended him from his horse just as the night rocked to a shot. Rabitoy squawked and hit hard on his shoulder. Fargo had no time to see if he was all right. Whirling, he palmed his Colt.

The trooper had turned and was running toward a saloon.

Fargo went after him. With a little luck he could wrap this up quickly. He came to the batwings to The Gold Spittoon.

Prudently, he poked his head over them before committing himself. A six-shooter blasted over near the bar and he nearly lost his hat. Ducking back, he heard curses and yells and the tromp of boots making for the rear of the establishment.

Fargo darted between the Spittoon and the next building. He flew to the back and again stuck his head out.

Four figures had just come out of the saloon and were fleeing to the west. "Stop!" he hollered, and again had to draw back as revolvers cracked and fireflies flared.

Crouching, Fargo leaped out and fired twice from the hip. There was a cry of pain and one of the four grabbed another to keep him from falling.

"Charlie's hit!"

The four turned into an alley.

Fargo swore and gave chase. He stopped short of the alley mouth and heard shouts and gunfire from the far end. Plunging in, he nearly tripped over someone sprawled at his feet.

It was the trooper he had shot. The man's hand rose and he weakly bleated, "Help me."

Fargo dropped to a knee. Almost too late he saw the man's other hand rise, holding a revolver. He swatted at it even as he jammed his Colt against the trooper's ribs, and fired.

The deserter cried out.

"You son of a bitch," Fargo said, snatching the revolver from his grasp.

"You've killed me, you bastard," the trooper growled, dark drops dribbling from the corner of his mouth.

"Don't expect tears," Fargo said.

"You miserable, rotten, stinking—" The trooper got no further. He stiffened and gasped and was gone.

"Good riddance." Fargo sprinted for Main Street. The shooting had stopped but a considerable ruckus was taking place. He burst out in time to spy three riders galloping away.

"Skye!" California Jim shouted. "Over here!"

It was Rabitoy. He was on his back in the middle of the street. Civilians had gathered, and as Fargo ran up one of them said, "The doc is on his way."

"How bad?" Fargo asked California Jim, but it was the lieutenant who answered.

"It hurts like hell but I think I'll live. Go after them. Don't let Mace and those others get away."

"We should stay with you, Lieutenant," California Jim said.

"No, damn it." Rabitoy grimaced. "Fargo, you go. Don't let them escape. I'm counting on you."

Fargo swore and sprinted to the Ovaro. Swinging up, he reined sharply around and used his spurs. The stallion took off as if shot from a cannon.

A side street loomed.

Fargo was flying past it when thunder crashed and lead sizzled near his ear. Drawing rein, he leaped down and palmed his Colt. He figured that Mace and the other two might be rattled by the death of their friend, and more willing to give up if given the chance. Cupping his hand, he hollered, "Luther Mace! Can you hear me?"

There was no reply.

"You've already lost one man," Fargo shouted. "Come out with your hands up before you lose another." He waited for an answer but they stayed silent. "Luther Mace! Can you hear me?"

An explosion of hooves warned him that the trio was on the move.

Fargo swore. He didn't go down the side street after them; he'd lose too much time. They were heading west so he did the same. If he could reach the end of Main Street before they reached the end of Second Street, they were as good as caught. He galloped past a saloon and a closed butcher shop and a closed bank and was almost to a millinery when two women came out of it and blundered into his path. Usually dress stores were closed at that hour. He hauled on the reins and the stallion dug in its hooves. The women were so near, Fargo was sure the Ovaro wouldn't stop in time but the stallion slid to a halt inches from the pair.

"My word!" a blonde exclaimed.

"You almost ran us down!" an older woman said in outrage. "Have you no common sense? The street is no place for reckless behavior."

Fargo reined around them and again resorted to his spurs. They hadn't delayed him much but any delay could cost him. Sure enough, when he came to the end of Main Street, the three deserters were clear of town and flying to the west on the only road.

Fargo did more swearing. He'd have to overtake them fast or they'd slip away in the dark. He lashed his reins and the stallion went flat out.

The dark shapes began to acquire substance and form. Without warning they veered off the road.

Fargo was fit to be tied. He veered after them and hadn't gone fifty yards when he once again drew rein. He couldn't hear them. He strained his ears but the night was quiet. He strained his eyes but beheld only ink.

"Where the hell did you get to?" he growled. He suspected they had stopped close by.

Quietly clucking to the stallion, Fargo roved in ever wider circles, seeking some sign of their presence.

It was half an hour before he admitted the truth—they'd gotten away.

Reluctantly, Fargo bent the Ovaro's hooves toward Hadleyville.

He didn't like to fail—at anything. It rankled, like a sore that wouldn't heal.

A lot of people were still out in Main Street.

Fargo stopped near some in front of The Gold Spittoon and said, "The officer and the other scout I was with?"

"Doc Baker's," a townsman in a derby replied, pointing. "It's the big house with the gables, on the right."

"I'm obliged."

"They gave you the slip, did they?" another man asked, and snickered.

Fargo was in no mood for idiots. "How would you like to be pistol-whipped?"

That ended the snickering.

Fargo rode on. He recognized California Jim and Rabitoy's mounts at a hitch rail. Drawing rein, he dismounted and walked up to a porch and knocked on the door.

A middle-aged woman bundled in a heavy robe and wearing a stocking cap answered. "Yes?"

"I'm with Lieutenant Rabitoy."

"Oh. Come in, please. You must be Mr. Fargo. They told me you might show up. I'm Mrs. Baker."

Fargo entered. A hall lamp glowed, and farther down light spilled from a room.

"I understand you went after some deserters," Mrs. Baker remarked. "Did you catch them?"

"They gave me the slip," Fargo admitted.

"That's too bad. They should honor the oath they take when they sign up. Some people have no honor."

"Ain't that the truth," Fargo said.

Mrs. Baker ushered Fargo to the lit room. "Have a seat, if you would. My husband is working on the young officer as we speak."

California Jim bounded up out of a chair and clapped Fargo on the arm. "You're back! Tell me you bucked those buzzards out in gore."

"I wish I'd stop being asked that," Fargo grumbled.

"Uh-oh."

"I did shoot one of them."

"That's something, anyway. The miserable bastards." Catching himself, California smiled at the physician's wife. "I'm sorry about my cussing, ma'am. It was a slip of the tongue."

"That's quite all right," Mrs. Baker said. "I've heard worse." She paused. "Can I get either of you anything? Coffee, perhaps? Or tea?"

"Coffee would be right fine," California Jim said. "I like mine black."

"How about you?" Mrs. Baker asked Fargo.

"I don't suppose you have some whiskey you could spare?"

Mrs. Baker sniffed. "I'm afraid not. The only liquor I allow in my house is for medicinal purposes."

"The night I've been having," Fargo said, "it figures."

3

To say that Colonel Williams wasn't pleased was an understatement. Seated in his chair, he drummed his fingers on his desk and said in pure sarcasm, "Well done, gentlemen."

Lieutenant Rabitoy squirmed. He was in full uniform, a bulge in his side where Doc Baker had applied a bandage. "If they hadn't shot me, I'm certain we would have caught them."

"That's a feeble excuse for someone who should know better," Colonel Williams said.

"Sir?"

"You heard me, Lieutenant. You handled it badly. You should not have let your presence be discovered until you were ready to take Private Mace and the others into custody."

"But, sir—" Rabitoy tried to get a word in.

"And what was that business with the gambler, Coltraine? Since when do we inject ourselves into civilian matters without express authorization?"

"He killed a man."

"A card cheat, from what I hear."

"Sir, that's no excuse for—" Rabitoy began.

Williams held up a hand. He was gray at the temples but hard as iron and carried himself like a man twenty years younger. "I don't want to hear another word about him. I want to discuss Private Mace. By all accounts, he was the instigator. He talked the others into deserting with him. And this isn't the first time."

"Is Mace even his real name?" California Jim asked.

"We're not sure," Colonel Williams said. "I'm highly doubtful. As you are all aware, some men make a career out of enlisting and staying in a while, then deserting and enlisting under an assumed name somewhere else."

"A stupid practice," Lieutenant Rabitoy muttered.

"A lucrative practice," Colonel Williams corrected him. "Each time they enlist they receive a bonus of a hundred dollars."

California Jim whistled.

"Exactly," Colonel Williams said. "Take a man like Mace. As best we can determine, he's deserted and reenlisted seven times."

"Seven!" Lieutenant Rabitoy blurted. "Why, that's seven hundred dollars."

"It explains why our desertion rate is up near fifteen percent a year," Colonel Williams said. "Most only reenlist once or twice. Mace and a few like him have made a career out of it."

"The army must be losing a heap of money," California Jim commented.

"That it is," Colonel Williams said. "And we intend to put a stop to it. To that end, we want to make an object lesson of Private Mace. The orders have come straight from Washington." Williams tapped a paper on his desk. "Mace is to be hunted down and brought up on charges. Once he's convicted, and there's absolutely no doubt he will be, he'll be flogged and confined to the stockade for five to ten years. It's hoped that his punishment will serve as a deterrent to others."

Fargo listened with mild interest. The desertion problem had little to do with him. He worked as a scout, nothing more.

Apparently California Jim was thinking the same thing because he asked, "Why are you telling us all this, Colonel? Why'd you call us in here?"

"You and Mr. Fargo are two of the best trackers we have," Williams replied. "We'd like for the two of you to devote yourselves entirely to Luther Mace. Track him down and bring him back and you'll have your government's gratitude."

California Jim glanced at Fargo and gestured as if to say, "Do you want to answer him or should I?"

Fargo cleared his throat. "Who came up with this brainstorm?"

"The idea to make an object lesson of Mace came from Washington, as I told you," Williams said. "I'm the one who would like to use you to bring it about. Why? Is there a problem?"

"Tracking a man down isn't the same as tracking hostiles or tracking game," Fargo said. "It's not really *tracking* at all."

"I agree," California Jim said. "A federal marshal would be better for something like this."

"I thought of that," Colonel Williams said. "But the marshals are stretched thin. The earliest they can have one here is in three or four weeks. And who knows where Mace will have gotten to by then?"

"Send your own troopers then," Fargo suggested.

"Again, I've considered doing so. And decided it's impractical. For one thing, most of them are young and green. They have no experience whatsoever in something like this."

"And we do?" California Jim said.

Williams nodded. "I think so, yes. Both of you are accomplished hunters. You go after your quarry and don't rest until you've brought it down. This won't be any different."

"Yes," Fargo said, "it will."

"You're my best option, gentlemen," Colonel Williams insisted. "But I feel it wouldn't be right to order you to do it. You must make the decision. You must volunteer. Talk it over and give me your decision in the morning."

"I know what mine is now," California Jim said.

"You'll be doing your country a favor," Colonel Williams stressed, "and help put a stop to a despicable deception that last year alone cost the government almost a quarter of a million dollars."

"That much?" California Jim marveled.

"It's obvious why the top brass want to nip the desertions in the bud, as it were."

"What it boils down to, though," California Jim said, "is that you're asking us to do law work without the badges. And we're not lawmen."

"For the duration you'll be acting under the authority of the U.S. Army's Provost Marshal's office," Colonel Williams said.

"What's that mean, exactly?"

Williams grinned. "You would be lawmen without badges. But I'll give each of you letters of authorization that will effectively give you carte blanche."

"Cart who?" California Jim said.

"It means you can basically do whatever you must in order to get the job done."

"I reckon we'll need to ponder on it some," California Jim said, with a nod at Fargo.

"Report here at eight in the morning and give me your decision."

Lieutenant Rabitoy asked, "What about me, sir? How am I involved?"

"You're not."

"Sir?"

"You'll rest up for a day and then resume your normal duties." Colonel Williams sat back. "That will be all, gentlemen."

California Jim waited until they were outside in the hot sun to ask Fargo, "What do you think, pard?"

Fargo shrugged. He didn't much like the idea but he couldn't come up with a reason to refuse. "I don't know yet."

He watched the sulking Rabitoy cross the parade ground. "What say we ride into Hadleyville and give it some thought over a few whiskeys?"

California chuckled. "I like how you go about making up your mind. We might as well do it lubricated."

The town was a ten-minute ride to the west. In the light of day it wasn't nearly as glamorous. A layer of dust gave the buildings a dreary look. The street was littered with droppings, and hogs, dogs, and even chickens were allowed to run free. The few folks moving about in the heat did so with the lethargy of turtles.

Fargo's favorite haunt was The Agate Saloon, named after the Agate River, which was another ten minutes west of Hadleyville.

At that time of the day the saloon was as lively as a funeral parlor between burials. A few men were at the bar, several more at the tables.

One man, in particular, drew Fargo's interest. He paid for drinks, handed one to California Jim, and nodded at the corner table. They drifted over.

"I took you for a night owl," Fargo said by way of greeting.

Jonathan Coltraine looked up from the cards he was shuffling. Across from him sat a townsman, sipping rum.

"Back in town again so soon?" the gambler said. "The army must not need much scouting done." He smiled and pushed an empty chair out with his foot. "Have a seat, you two. This here is Barnaby. He works at the general store."

Barnaby smiled.

Fargo eased down and took a sip of red-eye. The spreading warmth of the red-eye, combined with the tinkle of poker chips and the smell of tobacco, filled him with contentment. "No doves are around?"

Coltraine laughed. "All you ever think of is that pecker of yours. It's too early for them yet." He fanned the cards. "Which reminds me. How is that peckerwood of a lieutenant doing?"

"He'll live," California Jim said. "None the wiser, I'm sad to say."

"Some people are born with no common sense," Coltraine said. He glanced over at three men who had entered and were going to the bar.

"We've been asked to hunt down the deserters," Fargo mentioned by way of small talk.

"From what I hear," Barnaby the clerk remarked, "a lot of them pass through here."

Coltraine frowned.

"How's that again?" Fargo said. To his knowledge, Mace and his friends were the only ones to desert from Fort Barker in the past six months. He brought that up.

"Fort Barker isn't the only post in these parts," Barnaby reminded them. "There's Fort Kiley about a hundred or so miles to the south and Fort Sledgewick about the same distance to the north."

Fargo had been to both. It was unusual to have three forts so close together but the generals at the war department thought they would serve as a buffer between the hostiles and the settlers. The Indians, however, weren't intimidated; it just gave them more white invaders to kill.

"Wait," California Jim said. "Why would deserters from those other forts come through here?"

"I'm only repeating the rumor I've heard," Barnaby said. "I don't know if it's true."

Coltraine was staring at the three newcomers at the bar.

"Friends of yours?" Fargo said.

The three men had noticed Coltraine and were staring back.

All three were scruffy with stubble and dirty hair but they wore new store-bought clothes.

"See the one in the high hat?" Coltraine said.

Fargo nodded. The shortest wore a stovepipe, as well as a Remington high on his right hip and a bowie on the other. "He must wear that hat to make him feel taller."

"His name is Garrick. He happens to be the brother of the gent I shot last night. The other two are his cousins. The Pumas, they call themselves."

"That's their name?" California Jim said. "Honest to God?"

"So far as I know."

16

"I wish I had a name like Puma," California Jim said. "It beats mine all hollow."

"What's yours?" Barnaby asked.

"My last name is Morganstern."

"What's wrong with that?"

"My full name is Violet James Morganstern. My ma had her heart set on a girl and my pa let her use the name she'd picked on me. I dropped the Violet and the Morganstern and just use the James."

"I don't blame you," Barnaby said.

Fargo hadn't taken his eyes off the Pumas. As all three set down their empty glasses, he shifted and lowered his right arm to his side. "Here comes trouble."

4

Garrick Puma fancied himself. Where most men settled for drab clothes, he liked peacock hues. His shirt was red; his pants were blue. The legs were tucked into tooled leather boots with large silver spurs. In addition to the stovepipe, he wore a yellow bandanna and his gun belt was decorated with silver stars.

"Lord Almighty," California Jim breathed. "He's almost as handsome as me."

The other pair were cut from coarser muslin. The stubble and grime didn't enhance their looks any. One had a Smith & Wesson, the other a Colt on his left side worn lower than most men would wear one.

"The way they strut," California said, "I bet they provoke real easy."

Coltraine set down his cards and placed his hands flat on the table. "You gents want something?"

The short man in the stovepipe looked at Fargo and California and said, "I'm Garrick Puma."

"I know who you are," Coltraine said.

"These here are my kin, Lester and Puce," Garrick said, indicating the others.

"Puce Puma?" California Jim said, and chortled.

"You won't find it so damn funny in a minute," Puce told him.

Garrick's right thumb was hooked in his gun belt a few inches from his Remington. Sliding it closer, he said, "That was my brother you kilt last night."

"Know that, too," Coltraine said.

"We don't take kindly to what you done," Garrick said. "We don't take kindly to it at all."

"Chauncey was dumb," Coltraine said.

"We hear tell that you're goin' around sayin' he was cheatin' you," Garrick said.

"People need a reason," the gambler said.

"We don't like it," Garrick said, "you makin' him out to be no account."

Fargo finally spoke. "I'm not surprised."

Garrick's dark eyes flicked at him. "Who might you be? And what did you mean by that?"

California Jim said, "This here is Skye Fargo. Could be you've heard of him."

"Reckon I might have at that," Garrick said, not taking his eyes off Fargo. "You were in a shootin' match down to Missouri a while back with some of the best sharpshooters in the country. It was in the newspapers."

"Damn newspapers," Fargo said.

"Where do you stand in this?" Garrick asked.

Fargo nodded at Coltraine. "With him."

"Is that so?"

After about ten seconds of silence, the one called Puce said, "What are we waitin' for? Do we learn this gambler he can't go around shootin' Pumas or not?"

"Not," Garrick said.

Lester Puma said, "Ma will want the body but they went and buried him on Boot Hill."

Garrick looked at Coltraine. "Don't think this is over. There's a lot we'll stand for but not that."

The gambler rose. His frock coat was unbuttoned and his Colts were visible. "Whenever you want."

Just then there was a loud thump from over at the bar. The bartender had a shotgun. He wasn't pointing it in their direction but he didn't have to. "I own this establishment and I don't abide gunplay. Do I make myself clear?"

Garrick Puma said, "We hear you." He didn't sound concerned. Glaring at Coltraine, he wheeled. His cousins followed him out.

"Damned lunkheads," Coltraine said.

"Are they backshooters, do you reckon?" California Jim asked.

"It wouldn't surprise me."

It wouldn't surprise Fargo, either. He'd run into their kind more times than he cared to count. "Want to go after them and prod until they pull on us?"

"You'd do that for me?"

"I owe you for that time in Kansas," Fargo said, referring to a card game where a poor loser pulled a knife on him.

"All I did was yell a warning," Coltraine said.

"And saved me from a blade in the gut."

Coltraine moved toward the batwings. "I want to make sure they drifted off. I'll be right back."

"I like him," California said. "He doesn't take any guff, like someone else I know."

"Who?" Fargo said.

In a couple of minutes Coltraine was back. He sat and picked up his cards, saying, "Hadleyville is losing its appeal. I might drift down to New Orleans and spend time among civilized folks."

"Wish I could go with you," California Jim said. "I hear those New Orleans whores can curl a man's toes."

"And other parts."

"They can curl *that*?"

Fargo hadn't forgotten what they were talking about before the Pumas walked in. "Tell me more about the desertions," he said to Barnaby, who had been quiet the whole while. "What else have you heard?"

"Eh? Oh. Rumor has it there have been a lot of them, and that most of the deserters pass through Hadleyville."

"Why here?" California asked.

Fargo thought he knew. Anyone heading west would have to pass through Hadleyville to reach the ferry at the Agate River. Once across, it was a day's ride to the Wasatch Mountains, better known as the Mountains of No Return, and once over them, the deserters could head for parts unknown and never be found. He mentioned his notion.

"That would be my guess," Coltraine said, and wagged his cards. "Enough about the deserters. How about some poker? Got a few dollars you don't mind losing?"

"Listen to you," California said. "It could be we'll take yours."

For the next couple of hours Fargo relaxed and played and drank. As the afternoon waned the saloon filled and by sunset it was crowded.

Another townsman joined their table. Later, a farmer in a straw hat and bib overalls sat in.

Along about nightfall four doves sashayed from out of the back and were greeted with wolf howls and grins.

By then Fargo was over forty dollars to the better and in no hurry to return to the fort. His next hand he was dealt three twos, a queen and a king. He asked for two cards and got two nines. As he was calling, a warm hand brushed his neck and a sultry voice tinkled in his ear.

"What do we have here? How is it I haven't noticed you sooner, handsome?"

Fargo looked up.

She had tawny curls and strawberry lips and a twinkle in her green eyes. Her dress fit her so snug it left nothing to the imagination. Her perfume, her painted fingernails, her polished shoes lent her an aura of elegance.

"Name's Fargo," Fargo introduced himself.

"Mary Jane," the dove said, showing nice white teeth. "Pleased to make your acquaintance." She ran a finger along his ear. "Care to buy a girl a drink?"

"Care to hump me silly later?"

Mary Jane laughed. "Why, listen to you," she said in mock indignation. "Have you no shame?"

"No."

"Me either." Mary Jane bent and blew warm breath in his ear. "I might just take you up on that. But I don't get off until midnight."

"I'll be around."

Fargo bought her a whiskey. She brought him luck. He won the next several hands and was now close to a hundred dollars to the better.

Mary Jane drained her glass and frowned. "I'm afraid I have to mingle, handsome. You're on your own for a while."

As a coincidence, Fargo's luck turned when she walked off. The cards went against him, and he struggled to hold on to his winnings.

"I reckon I have to bow out for a bit," Coltraine unexpectedly declared. "I need to get a bite to eat."

Fargo's own stomach had been rumbling off and on. He hadn't had food since breakfast. "I'll tag along if you don't mind the company."

"How about your pard?"

"I'm staying," California said. "I'm overdue to win a few hands."

Main Street bustled with activity. Fargo and Coltraine walked half a block to a restaurant. It was run by a matron with hair as white as snow and the friendliness of a kitten.

Fargo ordered steak with all the trimmings. When a sizzling half-inch slab of beef was set in front of him, he dug in with relish. Onions and chopped peppers had been heaped on the steak and there was a side of mashed potatoes drowning in butter, and fresh peas. He asked and had five refills to wash the food down.

For Coltraine it was pork and a sweet potato and greens.

They were about done when a man in a derby entered and scanned the eaters and beamed as if he had struck the jackpot. Taking a pad and a pencil from his jacket, he came over. "Pardon me, sir," he said to Coltraine, "but you answer to the description I was given."

"No," the gambler said.

"You're not Jonathan Coltraine?"

"I am. And the answer is no."

The man uttered a nervous laugh. "I haven't introduced myself yet or explained why I'm here."

"You scribble for a living," Coltraine said.

"Why, as a matter of fact, I do. I work for the *Sledgewick Sentinel*. Hadleyville doesn't have its own newspaper so we cover both towns. I happened to hear about your shooting affray and wondered if I could have your side of the story?"

"I already gave you my answer. Twice."

"Couldn't you reconsider? I give you my word to write the truth and only the truth."

"That will be a novelty," Coltraine said.

"I don't understand why you're so unfriendly. I honest to God don't."

Fargo set down his coffee cup and waggled his finger. "Make yourself scarce."

The man stiffened. "Who are you to tell me what to do? I have every right to be here."

"And I have every right to chuck you through that front window."

The newspaperman's thin lips pinched and he let air out his nose. "Very well. I shouldn't disturb you gentlemen at your meal, I suppose. When would be a good time, Mr. Coltraine?"

"Ten minutes after I'm dead."

"You have a droll sense of humor, sir."

"And little patience."

The man stuck his pencil and pad in his pocket and bobbed his head and departed.

"Damn nuisances," Coltraine said. "Thanks for setting him back on his heels."

"Glad to," Fargo said, and meant it. It had been his experience that some so-called journalists wouldn't know the truth if it bit them on the ass.

They paid and went out. A welcome breeze had picked up, and a piano player was playing poorly.

"Nice night," Coltraine said.

Fargo turned to head for The Agate Saloon and the nice night exploded with gunfire.

5

Fargo's reaction was to drop flat. It saved his life. Slugs tore into the jamb and would have cored his chest had he been standing. Instantly, he palmed his Colt and sought the shooters.

Catty-corner from the restaurant stood a two-story hotel with a balcony on the second floor. Partially hidden by the hotel's sign, it was an ideal vantage point.

As if to prove him right, three rifles blasted at the top edge of the sign.

Fargo responded in kind. So did Coltraine.

People in the street were scattering. Men cursed and a few women screamed.

Heaving up, Fargo weaved as he ran and fanned two shots.

The men on the balcony let loose with another fusillade and dirt geysers spewed at his feet. He made it across the street and darted into the doorway of a barber shop. Hurriedly reloading, he sprang out and sped for the hotel. An overhang hid him. He was inside and crossing the lobby when he heard more shots from above. Taking the stairs three at a stride, he came to the second floor.

At the other end the door to the balcony was open and framed in the doorway was Puce Puma.

They fired at the same instant, and they both missed.

Fargo threw himself down and extended his arm to take aim and be sure but Puce was no longer there.

From outside came more shouts and shots.

Again Fargo pushed up. He burst onto the balcony to find it empty. A commotion drew him to the west end. Three figures were sprinting down the street. Even as he set eyes on them, one twisted and fired and the slug clipped the rail. He raised the Colt but the three ran around a hitch rail and put half a dozen horses between him and them.

Gripping the balcony rail, Fargo swung over. One-handed, he slid as low as he could go. His feet weren't more than seven or eight feet above the ground. Releasing his hold, he dropped and landed with a jolt but stayed upright and gave chase.

Coltraine was coming up the other side of Main Street, both Colts in his hands. "There they go!" he hollered.

Fargo saw them. They were swinging onto mounts. He aimed at the form under a stovepipe but Garrick swung onto the other side.

The next moment the three would-be assassins were galloping hell-bent out of Hadleyville.

Fargo ran to the Ovaro. He would be damned if he'd have a repeat of the night before; he used his spurs harder than was his habit. For half a mile the stallion pounded along the road to the west. Finally he drew rein and listened. The only sound was the Ovaro's breathing. He rose in the stirrups and peered intently along the road but nothing moved. "Damn." He sat there a few minutes, hoping in vain.

Fargo wasn't in the best frame of mind when he reined up at the hitch rail in front of The Agate Saloon. As he was climbing down, two familiar faces appeared out of the dark.

"They got away, I take it?" Coltraine said.

Fargo nodded.

"You should have given a yell," California Jim said. "I'd have gone with you."

"There wasn't time."

"Stinking bushwhackers," Coltraine said. "Now I have to hunt them down."

"Could be they'll light a shuck for who knows where," California Jim said, "and save you the trouble."

"I can't take the chance," Coltraine said. "I don't settle it, I'll be looking over my shoulder the rest of my days."

"Do they live hereabouts?" California asked.

"I see them in town fairly often. I'll ask around." Coltraine touched the brim of his black hat and went into the saloon.

California turned to Fargo. "Cat got your tongue, pard? You're uncommonly quiet."

"Two nights in a row I've let someone get away from me."

"We all have bad days. Look at the bright side. At least you're still breathing."

They went in. Fingers were pointed at Fargo and men whispered behind his back.

"You're the talk of the town," California Jim joked.

"If there's one thing in this life I can do without," Fargo said, "it's fame."

"Have you given any more thought to the colonel's proposition?"

"As a matter of fact, I did."

"Don't keep me in suspense."

"A man goes and deserts, it's between him and the army. And like you said, we're not lawmen."

"That means we're not?"

"But when a deserter takes a shot at me, that makes it personal."

"So that means we are? Which is it?" California said. "I'm confused as hell."

"I need to think on it more. But not now. I'm meeting a lady after a while."

"What she's got to do with whether we go after a bunch of deserters?"

"Not a thing," Fargo said. "I just want to dip my wick."

"Should have known," California Jim said.

Mary Jane and smiled and winked at Fargo as he shouldered to the bar. Coltraine was already at a poker table. Since there were no empty chairs, Fargo went to a table where there were. California joined him.

Fargo's first hand was a full house but after that the cards turned cold. He played cautiously until the feather touch of a finger on his earlobe let him know midnight had rolled around.

"I'm off work, handsome," Mary Jane playfully whispered. "And all yours."

"You don't say." Fargo grinned and pulled her into his lap. He inhaled her jasmine perfume and nuzzled her neck. "Let me finish this hand."

"Take however long you like," Mary Jane said. "I have all night."

Three jacks won Fargo the pot. He raked in his winnings, added them to his poke, and rose. "That will be all for me, gents." He nodded and grinned at California Jim, who was staring at Mary Jane's ample melons, and ushered her out into the night.

"Something wrong?" she asked when he moved out of the light spilling from inside and stood surveying Main Street from end to end.

Fargo wasn't expecting more trouble but it could be that Garrick Puma and his kin had circled back for another try. Only when his instincts assured him it was safe did he wrap his arm around

Mary Jane's waist and kiss her and say, "Your place or mine, and I don't have one."

Mary Jane laughed. "I've got a room. A rather nice one, if I say so myself."

She wasn't exaggerating. It was at the back of a boardinghouse, and she could come and go without disturbing the other boarders. There were two rooms, comfortably furnished. She opened a small cabinet and brought out a whiskey bottle and filled two glasses. Handing one to him, she raised hers and they clicked glasses.

"To making new friends," she said.

"To humping you silly," Fargo toasted. He gulped the Monongahela and put the glass on a table.

"That was fast," Mary Jane said. She'd taken a single sip. "I thought you might like to sit and talk a spell. It would help me relax."

"I have another way." Fargo cupped her bottom and hungrily pulled her to him.

"Oh my," Mary Jane teased. "Someone wants it bad." She stretched to put her glass on the table and then placed her hands on his shoulders. "Now, what do you have in mind, good sir?"

Their mouths fused and hers parted and their tongues met in a wet dance. Fargo's fingers sculpted her bottom and kneaded her back from her hips to her neck. Gradually he brought them around to her front. When he cupped her breasts she gasped and ground her hips against him.

"You sure do excite me."

They went on kissing and caressing, and Fargo's pants bulged. Scooping her into his arms, he carried her into the bedroom and discovered a four-poster bed with a canopy. "You like to do it in style," he said.

Mary Jane took her lips from his neck to say, "It came with the place. It's one of the reasons I took the rooms."

Fargo eased her down. He undid his gun belt and removed his spurs and stretched out beside her. She eagerly pressed into him and they resumed where they had left off. Her fingers were everywhere. She knew how to arouse a man, and then some. When her fingers slid low on his pants, it was his turn to gasp.

"Like that, do you?"

"Like it a lot," Fargo growled.

"I can tell."

Peeling her dress took a while. At the back were stays and a row of tiny buttons that Fargo nearly tore off in annoyance.

He finally got it down around her waist and devoted himself to her globes. They were glorious; full, and arched, and tipped with long nipples that were a delight to suck on and pinch.

She cooed and squirmed, one hand in his hair, the other doing things to him below his belt.

Presently, he had the dress off and sat back to admire her. With her hair disheveled and her full breasts swollen and that hungry look in her hooded eyes, she was a hot cherry pie he couldn't wait to taste.

"Like what you see?" she husked.

"Beats looking in a mirror," Fargo said.

"Not from where I lay, you good-looking devil, you."

Mary Jane got his shirt and his pants off and ran her hand over his washboard midriff. "Goodness. You have more muscles than most."

"I have this, too," Fargo said, and placed her hand on his member.

"Hello, stallion," Mary Jane said. She commenced to lightly stroke him.

Fargo grit his teeth and tried not to go over the brink too soon. He rubbed and molded and kissed, and eventually he was ready. Parting her thighs, he slid the tip of his pole along her slit. Mary Jane shivered. He penetrated a couple of inches, and she moaned. He rammed in all the way and her eyes grew wide and she wrapped her legs tight around him and said, "Do me. Do me hard."

Fargo was happy to oblige. He gripped one of the bedposts and drove up and in with the tireless pace of a steam engine piston. Under them, the bed bounced and creaked.

"Yes," Mary Jane exclaimed. "Oh, yes."

Fargo winced when her teeth dug into his shoulder. Her nails raked his back. She liked to draw blood, this one. He rammed harder and she bit harder. Soon both of them were at a fever pitch.

Mary Jane gushed first. She arched her back and her mouth parted but the only sound she uttered was a tiny mew of raw pleasure.

Fargo went on pounding her but not for long. A keg of black powder went off between his legs and he about lifted her into the air with the violence of his thrusts. The whole bed shook and rattled, and it was a wonder it didn't break. Eventually he coasted to a stop and lay spent and sweaty and content.

Between the earlier excitement and the full meal and now this, Fargo felt fatigue creep over him. He closed his eyes. He figured he would sleep a while, collect California Jim, and head back to the fort.

"Hey now," Mary Jane said, poking him in the side. "Don't you fall asleep on me. I'd like a second helping." She grinned and poked him. "Maybe a third if you're up to it."

"Oh hell," Fargo said.

6

"What did you decide?" Colonel Williams asked when Fargo and California Jim entered his office the next morning.

"I don't know yet," California Jim replied.

"You haven't made up your mind?" The colonel sounded disappointed.

California jabbed a thumb at Fargo. "He ain't told me what we're going to do."

"So that's how it is," Williams said.

"What *did* we decide?" California Jim asked.

"We'll take the job," Fargo announced, "so long as we're free to do as we see fit."

"Within limits you are," Colonel Williams said. "You'll be under army jurisdiction and expected to abide by all pertinent rules and regulations."

California said, "That sounds to me like we're on a leash."

"I don't see why you're making an issue of this," Colonel Williams told him.

"All I need to know," Fargo said, "is that if these deserters try to put holes in us, the army won't be mad if we put holes in them."

"You're entitled to defend yourselves, yes."

"Then there's just one more thing," Fargo said, and made a teepee of his hand. "Why didn't you tell us that desertions are up at all the forts in this area?"

"Who told you that?"

"A little bird," Fargo said. "True or not?"

"Unfortunately, it's true," the officer confirmed. "It started about a year ago. Here at Fort Barker and at Fort Sledgewick and Fort Kiley. Counting Mace and those who left with him, it brings the total to twenty-four."

"Tarnation," California Jim said. "That's a lot."

"It's more than normal. And the strange thing is, none of the three forts are hellholes. I'd understand it if that were the case. But as you've seen for yourselves, I treat my men with respect, and the

onditions are as comfortable as I can reasonably make them. The
ame with the commanders at Sledgewick and Kiley."

"So there's no reason for all these troopers to up and skedad-
le?" California Jim said.

"Not to my mind."

"We'll find the answer," Fargo said, "but it might take a while."

"Take all the time you need," Colonel Williams said. "When do
ou want to start?"

"Right this minute." Fargo stood and they shook hands. "Don't
ret any if you don't hear from us. We'll be off in the wilds."

"Good luck," Williams said, "to both of you."

Troopers were drilling on the parade ground and from the black-
mith's came the clang of hammer and steel. Up on the ramparts
entries paced.

"We're not mounting up?" California Jim said when Fargo
valked past the hitch rail in front of headquarters.

"We're paying the sutler a visit."

"Good idea. We can stock up on grub."

"What little we need we already have," Fargo said. "We're good
t living off the land."

"Then why see the sutler?"

Fargo should have thought it was obvious. Sutlers were civil-
an merchants allowed to run stores on military posts. They sold
verything under the sun, and were known as "a trooper's best
riend."

This particular sutler was called Simmons. A swarthy man
vith curly black hair and a bushy mustache, he was hardly ever
een without his apron on. At the moment he was helping a middle-
ged woman choose material for a dress and said to Fargo and
California Jim, "I'll be with you in a moment, gentlemen."

The woman looked at them and frowned.

It reminded Fargo that scouts didn't enjoy the best of reputa-
ions. Opinion had it that his kind drank too much and whored too
nuch and bathed too little. In his case, two of the three were true.
"We're not in any hurry."

"We're not?" California Jim said.

Fargo went down the aisle to the pickle barrel and sat on it and
olded his arms.

California was more interested in the jars of hard candy. He practically watered at the mouth as he stuck his nose to each jar and made mewing sounds like a ten-year-old.

"I forgot you have a sweet tooth," Fargo said.

"It's my ma's fault."

"She fed you a lot of sweets when you were little?"

"She didn't feed us enough. We were lucky to get one pie a month. And I could count the cakes she made on one hand and have fingers left over. As for candy—" California sadly shook his head. "She claimed sugar was bad for us. Can you believe it?" He opened a jar of raspberry sticks, slid one out, and stared at it as if it were a rare jewel. "Have you ever seen anything so delicious in all your born days?"

"Pussy," Fargo said.

California roared but fell silent when Simmons came to the counter with the woman in tow.

"What's so funny?" the sutler asked.

"Uhhhh—" California Jim looked at the woman and blushed from his neck to his hairline.

"I told him a joke." Fargo came to his rescue.

"A risqué joke, I'd warrant," the woman said in disapproval. She had a square face on a stout neck and a body that could be described only as oxlike.

"Risk-who?" California Jim said.

"She means it was dirty," Fargo said, and smiled at her. "It's about a corset salesman and three farmer's daughters. Would you care to hear it?"

"I certainly would not."

"It mainly has to do with corncobs," Fargo said, "and all the ways they can be put to use."

Now it was the woman who blushed. "I never," she said indignantly.

"You should." Fargo smiled innocently. "It helps clear the nose."

Simmons said, "That will be enough talk about corncobs and such. I'm surprised at you, Fargo. I thought you had more respect for ladies than that."

"I do," Fargo said. "Which is why the farmer's daughters use the cob on the salesman and not the other way around."

The woman puffed out her bosom, snatched her material, and wheeled and stomped out. She made it a point to slam the door after her.

"I should be mad but I'm not," Simmons said. "Mrs. McGillicutty isn't known for her sense of humor."

"She's probably known for her big ass," California Jim said.

Simmons laughed. "Seriously, gentlemen. I can't have you driving off my customers like that."

"We'll get out of your hair," Fargo said, "as soon as you tell us everything you've heard about the desertions."

"Excuse me?"

Fargo motioned at the shelves crammed with merchandise.

"A man like you hears a lot about what's going on at a post. What's the latest on the deserters?"

"There isn't any, that I'm aware," Simmons said. "It's not something the soldiers here are proud of. Or their families, for that matter."

"You haven't heard a thing?"

Simmons pursed his lips and scratched his chin. "Well, gossip has it that desertions are up—"

"We know that," California Jim said.

"—not just here but at Fort Kiley and Fort Sledgewick."

"We know that, too."

"It started about a year ago—"

"Know that."

"—and the last were a trooper by the name of Mace and three others."

"Know, know, know," California Jim said.

"Then why the hell are you asking me?" Simmons said.

"That's all?" Fargo prodded.

"Word is that all the deserters headed west," Simmons threw in.

"That's no surprise," Fargo brought up. "Once over the mountains they can go anywhere."

"True," Simmons said. "But some of them were from back east and never returned home."

"You know this for a fact?"

"Again, it's only rumor. You should be aware of it. You're a scout, for crying out loud."

"What's west of here that would interest them so much?" California Jim wondered.

"I reckon we'll have to find out." Fargo got up off the pickle barrel. "Anything else?"

"Just Jackson."

"Who?"

"Arvil Jackson. He was from Tennessee, I think. He deserted with two others about eight months ago. Everyone had about forgotten about them when Jackson came crawling up to the gate one night."

"Crawling?" California Jim said.

Simmons nodded. "He had on torn pants and nothing else. His feet were bloody and raw." Simmons shook his head. "The poor bastard had been beaten within an inch of his life. So many welts and bruises, I couldn't bear to look at him."

"Injuns maybe?" California said.

"That's what a sergeant asked but Jackson said it wasn't redskins. Jackson opened his mouth to say more, and died."

"I'll be damned," California Jim said. "Why didn't the colonel tell us?"

Fargo shrugged. "Maybe he didn't think it was important enough."

"He should," Simmons said. "Jackson said something as he was giving up the ghost."

"What was it?" California Jim excitedly asked.

"The Mountains of No Return."

"That makes sense. We know they head that way anyway."

"Which if you ask me is the biggest mistake they could make. Hell, even the Utes don't like to go in there."

"Is that all you've heard?" Fargo asked.

"All that I remember." Simmons started to turn away and stopped. "Oh. Wait. They found a slip of paper in Jackson's pocket. It had one word on it. *Agate.*"

"Agate what?" California said. "The river? The saloon? The feed and grain that has the name?"

"How would I know?" Simmons said. "No one could figure it out. Not the colonel, not the junior officers, not anyone."

California looked at Fargo. "What do you think it means?"

"We'll find out together."

"It sure is a puzzle," California said. "More deserters than ever, and all of them head west even when a lot are from the east. And then one shows up near dead with the word *Agate* on him. If that makes any kind of sense, I'll eat my hat."

Fargo held out his hand to the sutler. "I'm obliged."

"Glad I could help, what little it was." Simmons paused. "One more thing. I don't know if it's important but I neglected to mention it when I told you about Jackson. They didn't just beat on him."

"I won't even try to guess," California said.

"They cut off his ears."

California's throat bobbed up and down. "That settles it. It had to be Injuns." He turned to Fargo. "You're not saying a hell of a lot. Doesn't this spook you any?"

"Not as much as it could."

"How so?"

"They could have cut off his pecker."

7

Coltraine was finishing his breakfast at the restaurant when Fargo and California Joe strode in the next morning.

The gambler looked up and grunted. "Getting up this early should be against the law." His face was drawn and his eyes were bloodshot.

"Too much red-eye last night?" California asked.

"Not enough," the gambler said.

Fargo pulled out a chair and ordered a coffee. He'd had some at the fort but more wouldn't hurt, not with the ride they had ahead.

California said, "Skye told me about us combining forces, as it were."

"I have the Pumas to hunt down and you have your deserters," Coltraine said. "And where we're going it won't be a picnic."

"Ain't that the truth," California said. "There's been reports of the Utes acting up. Young bucks out to make a name for themselves by counting coup."

Fargo had been into the Wasatch Range on several occasions. Situated well north of the beaten tracks to Oregon Country and California, it was largely uninhabited by whites. Unlike to the west and the south of the range, where thousands of Mormons had settled, this part of Utah Territory was remote and wild and perilous as hell. In the early days it had been home to trappers and mountain men and some were still around. And now there were a few small towns like Hadleyville.

"I'm not looking forward to this," Coltraine said. "Cramping my ass on a horse for ten hours a day isn't my idea of a good time."

"You'd rather be in a chair playing cards," California teased.

"Hell yes." Coltraine forked the last piece of egg on his plate and emptied his cup with a swallow. "My horse and the pack animal are over to the livery."

"You're sure going to a lot of trouble over these Pumas," California mentioned.

"I know their kind. And I refuse to be looking over my shoulders the rest of my days."

"You could go somewhere else. I doubt they'd follow you to Denver or New Orleans."

"Did you forget they tried to gun me down?"

"So you're out for a reckoning," California said.

"Wouldn't you be?"

Hadleyville was stirring to life. Stores were opening and saloons were being swept out. A teller in the bank was raising the shades.

Fargo idly wondered if the town would still exist in five years. Many a settlement had dried up for a lack of customers to keep the merchants in business, and unless gold or silver was found in the Wasatch Mountains to lure in a greedy horde, he could see Hadleyville withering and dying and becoming just another ghost town.

It wasn't quite eight o'clock when they rode out along the road to the west. They passed a few hardscrabble farms and then a few cabins and after that there was nothing but rolling hills until they came to the Agate River and the ferry.

The Agate was narrow and deep and the current so strong that fording it was a risk in itself. At a point where it widened and slowed, a man by the name of Milner had built a log house for his family with a tavern attached for travelers and then built the ferry and charged to get across.

Two horses were at the tavern hitch rail; ponies with plain saddles and parfleches for saddlebags.

"Mountain men," California guessed.

"Or trappers," Fargo said.

"One and the same to me," Coltraine chimed in.

California grinned and smacked his lips. "How about we wet our whistles before we cross? Just one drink, pard, to get us through the day?"

Fargo didn't mind. It would be a while before they had whiskey again. He alighted and looped the Ovaro's reins and went in.

The tavern was narrow and dark with only a few tables and a long bar. A pair of bearded hulks in buckskins were at one of the tables, drinking. Each had a rifle on the table next to him, and each had a knife in a hip sheath. One also had a tomahawk stuck under his belt.

The bartender was a pleasant surprise. She was young and shapely with long auburn hair spilling over slender shoulders. "How do you do," she greeted them with a smile. "I'm Edith Milner. My pa owns this place. There's rooms at the back if you want to stay the night."

"Hell, girl," California said, "it's still morning. Who stops this early?"

"You never know," Edith said. She hadn't taken her blue eyes off Fargo. "And you, sir? Can I interest you in a drink?"

"That, and a lot more," Fargo responded.

"Here we go," California said.

Coltraine laughed.

Fargo leaned on the bar and asked for a glass of Monongahela. "I'd also like some information."

"My bust is thirty-eight," Edith said with a grin.

California nudged Coltraine. "How does he do it? Women never come right out with it to me."

"You're uglier."

"Thanks a heap."

Fargo rested his forearms on the bar. "The information I'm after has to do with soldiers."

"You'll find a lot of them at Fort Barker," Edith said mischievously.

"I just came from there," Fargo revealed. "I'm after deserters. Three came this way the night before last. A man who goes by the name of Mace and two others. Did you happen to see them?"

"Night before last?" Edith shook her head. "My brother was taking his turn to tend bar. I was in the house with my ma and my little sister."

Coltraine broke in with, "How about last night? Did Garrick Puma and his cousins stop in?"

"I don't know anyone by that name," Edith said.

"That's peculiar," the gambler said. "They've hung around these parts a while now. And from what I hear, they go in and out of the Wasatches a lot."

"Could be they do," Edith said. "It doesn't mean I've ever met them."

One of the men in buckskins, the one with the tomahawk, looked up. "I hear that right, stranger? You're lookin' for the Puma clan?"

"I sure as hell am," Coltraine said.

"It's a big 'un," the mountain man said. "Twenty or thirty or better."

"You know this how?" Coltraine asked.

The man nodded at his partner. "Me and Eb, here, trap for a livin'. We don't get down to the low country much. Now and then when we do, we go by Puma Valley, as they call it."

"They've got a bunch of homesteads," Eb said, "so far back in, they ain't got any neighbors for fifty miles."

California asked, "Are they friends of yours?"

"Not hardly," the first mountain man said. "They tend to stick to themselves."

"Which is fine by us," Eb said. "We don't like people much anyhow. Do we, Arvil?"

"We sure don't," Arvil agreed.

Since the pair were being so talkative, Fargo had a question of his own. "Have you two seen any deserters up your way?"

Arvil laughed. "As high up as we live, all we ever see are bears and elk and such."

"How about Utes?" California Jim asked. "You see much of them?"

"We try to see them before they see us," Eb joked. "We're partial to our hair."

"And we don't see 'em too often," Arvil said. "We live in a part of the mountains that their tribes think is bad medicine."

"On purpose," Eb said.

"Smart, ain't it?" Arvil said, tapping his temple. "Don't you think?"

"It keeps you alive," Fargo said.

"No offense, gents," Coltraine said, "but living in the middle of nowhere without creature comforts isn't my idea of living." He sipped and added, "Give me a saloon and good drink and good food and a soft bed to sleep in."

"I take it by your garb that you're a card shark," Arvil remarked.

"I'm honest at my trade," Coltraine said.

Eb grinned. "No offense, either, but that makes you mighty rare. Most of the gamblers I've met would rig a game with their own ma."

Fargo figured that Coltraine would be insulted but the gambler chuckled.

"I've met more than a few of those myself."

"One thing you should know," Eb said, turning serious. "Those Pumas? They're snake-mean. You go anywhere near their neck of the woods and they come bustlin' out with their rifles and shotguns."

"Leave it to me to kill one of them," Coltraine said.

"You did what now?" Arvil said.

"I shot Chauncey Puma."

"I'm surprised the others haven't come after you."

"Some of them did."

Arvil scratched his beard. "And now you're headin' up after them?"

"That ain't too bright," Eb said.

Fargo was struck by a thought. "These Pumas. You say they live pretty far back in?"

"Farther than anyone else," Eb confirmed.

"Do they trap for a living?"

Arvil laughed. "Not that bunch. I don't know as they do anything other than lie around and drink."

"Laziest folks you ever did see," Eb said.

Just then the door opened and in came a burly man wearing a coat and a cap. It was the ferryman, Milner. He came over and went around the bar and filled a glass.

"Ma better not catch you," Edith said. "It's not even noon yet."

"Hush, child. I'm a grown man. I can do as I please." Milner glanced at a door at the back of the room, and took a quick gulp. Then he faced around. "Are you gents fixing to cross anytime soon? If not, I've got chores to tend to. You can give a holler when you're ready."

"Five to ten minutes," Fargo said. That would give them time to finish their drinks.

"I'll be waiting." Milner took another gulp and went out.

"We're headin' up into the high country, too," Arvil revealed.

"We're comin' back from sellin' furs in Hadleyville," Eb said. He grinned and winked. "And havin' a high time with a couple of painted ladies."

"They were wonderful friendly," Arvil said.

The ferry was tied at the end of a short ramp used to load wagons and animals. Fargo led the Ovaro up to it. Across the river, beyond a few hills, rose the Wasatch Range; stark, towering, and foreboding.

California Jim was at his side, and coughed. "The Mountains of No Return. I hope we make it back in one piece."

"You and me, both," Fargo said.

8

The trails into the mountains were few. From the ferry landing on the west side of the river, one trail meandered generally north, another wound to the northwest, a third to the southwest.

None saw a lot of use. They weren't rutted by wagon tracks. Along some stretches the ground was so hard that horses left little sign. It took an experienced eye to follow them.

Fargo had an experienced eye. He could read sign where others couldn't. The trail they wanted was the one to the northwest.

California Jim was behind him, then Coltraine, leading the pack animal.

They had climbed steadily for more than an hour when Fargo came to a bench and drew rein. He waited for his companions to join him to announce, "We're being followed."

"I noticed that my own self," California confirmed.

The gambler rose in his stirrups and gazed back down the trail. "I haven't seen anyone."

"I don't know who it is yet," Fargo said, "but there are two of them."

"Could be Arvil and Eb," California said.

"They took the trail to the north," Coltraine noted. "We all saw them."

"We saw them start up it," Fargo amended.

California nodded. "It would have been easy for them to circle back or cut across."

"Why would they follow us?" Coltraine asked. "They seemed friendly enough."

"We'll find out when they get tired of shadowing us," Fargo said.

"We shouldn't let them pick when and where," California advised.

"My thinking exactly." Fargo gigged the Ovaro and climbed for another half an hour before he came to a spot that suited him.

It was a notch in a ridge. The trail went through it and down the

41

other side. About thirty yards wide, the facing slopes were too steep for a horse, and heavily timbered.

Fargo halted and said, "This will do." Dismounting, he shucked his Henry from the saddle scabbard and worked the lever to feed a cartridge into the chamber.

"You shouldn't do it alone," California said.

Fargo handed him the Ovaro's reins. "Go on with Jon. Not too far. If you hear shots, come on the run."

"You're lying in wait for them?" Coltraine stated the obvious.

"We can't have someone on our back trail the whole way."

"If it is those two mountain men, odds are they're up to no good," California said.

"Odds are," Fargo agreed.

California and the gambler kept going.

Fargo watched until they were out of sight and then he entered the woods. Only a few yards in was a spruce with a wide trunk. He sat with his back to it and the Henry across his lap.

A jay screeched at him but lost interest and flew off. A squirrel scampered in the high branches. A pair of finches alighted but didn't stay long.

Fargo heard the clomp of hooves before he saw them.

Frowning, he rose into a crouch. When the pair were abreast of him he stepped into the open and leveled his rifle. "Small world," he said.

Arvil was in the lead and had his eyes on the ground. Eb was staring ahead. Both had Sharps rifles across their saddles.

They weren't spooked or alarmed by Fargo's sudden appearance. Reining up, they both smiled.

"Howdy again, friend," Arvil said.

"What are you doin' here?" Eb asked.

"I could ask you the same thing," Fargo responded. "And I am."

"We're on our way up into the high country," Arvil said. "You know that."

"I know you took the north trail and now here you are on this one," Fargo said.

"We talked it over and decided we should lend you a hand," Arvil glibly claimed.

"That's right," Eb said, nodding. "There's a lot of them Pumas and only three of you."

"You're right neighborly," Fargo said.

Arvil shifted and looked at Eb. "He sounds as if he doesn't believe us."

"I suppose I wouldn't, was I in his boots," Eb said.

Arvil shifted even more. Each degree of turn brought the muzzle of his Sharps more toward Fargo. "I don't know as I like bein' suspicioned."

"Well, he hardly knows us." Eb played his good-natured part.

"The only thing I want to know," Fargo said, "is if all that talk at the tavern was true."

"Now you're sayin' we might be liars?" Arvil shifted more as he spoke. The muzzle of his Sharps was now only a short sweep from pointing at Fargo.

"I'm saying," Fargo said, "that you're piss poor at this. Are you on your own or are your last names Puma?"

"We're no kin of that bunch," Eb said. "And every word we said about them was true."

"They're vermin," Arvil declared. "And what are you?" Fargo said.

"Use to be," Eb said wistfully, "we could make our livin' by trappin' and nothin' else. Those were grand days." A dreamy expression came over him. "Prime peltries brought top dollar. A man could make in a season what most folks earn in a whole year." He sighed. "But plews don't count for much these days. And we still have to buy supplies and ammunition and such."

"It doesn't need to be like this," Fargo said. "Turn around and go back down."

"Ain't you kind," Arvil said.

"It's your horses and guns," Eb said. "They'd fetch a lot of money."

"A lot of money," Arvil echoed.

"It's not worth dying over," Fargo said.

Eb's expression grew sorrowful. "I'm sorry, mister. We made up our minds and we have it to do."

Arvil nodded. "We've been in tight situations before and we've always made it through."

"Last chance," Fargo said.

Arvil glanced at Eb and Eb nodded, and Arvil swung his Sharps at Fargo and Fargo shot him in the chest. Arvil reacted as if he'd been punched. His sorrel reared. Fargo turned to bring his Henry to bear on Eb but Eb had slipped over the other side of his mount and was hanging, Comanche-style, by a forearm and an ankle. Eb's animal broke into motion, going past Arvil's horse on the side away from Fargo.

Arvil was still in the saddle. A look of intense concentration on his face, he took deliberate aim.

Fargo shot him again.

Arvil swayed and his Sharps dipped but, incredibly, he clenched his teeth and raised his Sharps.

Fargo shot him in the head.

By then Eb's animal was galloping for the timber on the other side of the notch.

Fargo sighted down the barrel but he couldn't see enough of Eb to take the shot. He cursed himself for not keeping the Ovaro close by. Now Eb would get away.

Arvil was oozing to earth like so much mud. His Sharps fell from fingers gone lifeless and clattered on the ground.

Fargo kept his Henry on Eb's horse until the trees swallowed it. He smothered an urge to run after it. He couldn't catch it on foot.

Hooves drummed to the west, and California Jim and Coltraine came hurrying to help, California tugging on the Ovaro's reins.

Arvil was upside down, his leg somehow caught, Fargo moved to dislodge him and the horse pranced away, Arvil's arms flapping like a bird's wings. Fargo moved faster and so did the horse.

"Catch that damn lunkhead," he hollered.

California let go of the Ovaro's reins and veered to comply.

Coltraine came to a stop. "I'll be damned," he said, staring after Arvil. "It was them, after all."

"They weren't as they seemed," Fargo said. Not much in the mountains would be. The people, that was. The animals were another matter; they were always true to their natures.

"I never thought I'd see the day where I was too trusting," Coltraine said.

"They were good at pretending."

"Still, I thought I could read people. At the tables I do it all the time and I do it well."

So did Fargo. But he also did something the gambler didn't; he spent a lot of his time in the wilds, where it paid to distrust strangers until they proved they were worth trusting.

California had headed off the sorrel and was bringing it back, Arvil still hanging upside down.

"Where did his partner get to?" Coltraine wondered as he bent to climb down. It saved his life. There was a thunderous boom from the timber that Eb had vanished into, and Coltraine's hat flipped into the air.

"Get to cover!" Fargo shouted. He darted to the Ovaro and was in the saddle in a twinkling. Twisting, he fired at the woods, not one shot but five in swift succession. He didn't have a target. He sprayed the lead to discourage Eb.

The gambler was racing toward the trees on the other side of the notch.

California was trying to get there, too, but the sorrel balked. It dug in its hooves and refused to be budged. He tugged furiously on the reins.

There was another clap of thunder and the reins parted.

"Run for it!" Fargo yelled.

California slapped his legs, bending low so he'd be harder to hit.

Fargo made it to the forest on the other side without being shot at.

A piercing whistle rose from the opposite woods and Arvil's sorrel moved toward them.

"He's more interested in his partner than in us," Coltraine said.

Which was good for them, Fargo reflected. Eb had missed blowing the gambler's head off by a hair, and had shot the reins to Arvil's animal from a good twenty yards away. That was some shooting.

California swore. "Damn them, anyhow. Why'd they have to go and be dishonest?"

Fargo was hoping for a glimpse of Eb. The sorrel came to the edge of the far trees and stopped but Eb didn't rush out to claim it.

"Do we go after him?" Coltraine asked.

"You ever seen the size of the hole a Sharps can blow in you?" California said.

"It could be this will end it," Fargo said. "Eb will take his pard's body and go."

"Or it could make him so mad, he won't rest until we're buzzard bait."

Fargo spied a hand reaching out of the greenery toward the sorrel. Fingers snagged what was left of the reins and pulled the sorrel from sight.

"Sneaky cuss," California said.

They waited in silence. The birds had gone quiet and not so much as a chipmunk stirred.

Finally Eb gave a holler. "Do you hear me over there, you fellers?"

"We hear you," Fargo answered.

"Is it over?" California shouted. "Have you learned your lesson and you'll leave us be?"

"Mister," Eb returned, "I aim to see all of you in hell."

9

That was the last they heard from him.

California shouted a few times, trying to get Eb to talk, but he didn't respond.

Half an hour went by. It was Fargo who spotted the trapper well down the mountain, leading Arvil's horse with the body draped over the saddle. He pointed. "There he goes."

"Like I said," California grumbled, "he's a damned sneaky cuss. Now we'll have him on our back trail the rest of the way. And him with a Sharps. If he's any kind of shot, he can pick us off from a quarter-mile away."

"Just what I needed to hear," Coltraine said.

"Or I can go after him and end it," Fargo proposed.

"Why you alone?" California asked.

"Less chance of him spotting only one of us." And, Fargo could be a sneaky cuss too when he had to be.

"I don't know," California Jim said. "We're pards and pards should stick together."

"And I don't need a nursemaid," Coltraine said, "if that's what you're thinking."

"I wasn't." Fargo stepped to the Ovaro and shoved the Henry into the saddle scabbard. Gripping the saddle horn, he swung up and hooked his boot in the opposite stirrup. "Find a spot with water and make camp. If I'm not back in two days, you're on your own."

"I don't like it," California said.

Fargo tapped his spurs. He stayed in the trees, paralleling the trail. Time and again he rose in the stirrups, seeking a glimpse of Eb. He didn't spy him anywhere. He began to wonder if Eb had stopped to bury Arvil. Then, toward the middle of the afternoon, the mountain man came out of the forest still leading the horse with the body and still heading lower.

Fargo closed in.

Eb wasn't in any particular hurry. Apparently he was convinced no one was after him. He descended to a meadow and dismounted. Going into the woods, he was soon back with a thick broken limb and commenced to dig. He scooped a shallow grave, and when he was done, he took a flask from a parfleche and squatted and sipped, staring glumly at the body.

Fargo felt no regret. It had been Arvil or him. The pair were murdering bastards who befriended people heading up into the high country, and then hunted them down and killed them. It was cutthroats like these two who gave the Wasatch Range its nickname of the Mountains of No Return.

Eb must have downed half the flask when he capped it and hauled his dead friend to the grave and rolled the body in. He went through Arvil's pockets and stripped Arvil of his sidearm and knife and everything else. Eb covered him with dirt and piled brush and limbs on top. When he had heaped a small mound, he stepped back and stood with his head bowed.

By then Fargo had worked around the meadow. He tied the Ovaro to a fir and shucked the Henry and cat-footed up behind Eb as silently as a stalking Apache. He waited until Eb sighed and unfolded his hands to say, "We meet again."

Eb glanced over his shoulder, then at his Sharps, which he'd left on the ground a few feet away. "This is embarrassin'," he said, and raised his arms.

"You can go for your rifle if you think you can make it," Fargo said.

Eb's eyebrows knit, and he smirked. "I'll be damned. You can't shoot a man in the back. Ain't that decent of you?"

Fargo didn't reply.

"If all I do is stand here, what then?" Eb taunted.

"You won't," Fargo said.

"Why not?"

"It's not in you to do nothing."

"You think you know me but you don't," Eb scoffed.

"I know your kind," Fargo said.

"If you do you are one up on me," Eb said. "I've never savvied men like you. To me, killin' a person is no different than shootin' a deer or a grouse."

"It wouldn't be," Fargo said.

"It's all that 'Thou shalt not kill' nonsense," Eb said. "It gives folks the mistaken notion that they should bawl like a baby over somethin' that comes natural."

"Natural to you."

"And you," Eb said. "I can see it in your eyes. You only pretend to be civilized."

"Go for a gun," Fargo said. "Your rifle or your pistol, either will do."

"I'm not stupid," Eb said.

"Sure you are," Fargo said, "or you and Arvil wouldn't have done what you did."

"Killin' folks for their possibles, you mean?" Eb snorted. "It's no different than droppin' an elk for the meat."

Fargo was idly curious. "How many did you and your pard do in?"

Eb shrugged. "I never bothered to count 'em. Fifteen to twenty, I reckon. Only a few were women and kids." He glanced at the Sharps again.

Fargo was content to bide his time. Plenty of daylight was left.

"Speakin' of sendin' folks to hell," the mountain man said, "the Pumas will do you and your friends in, you go after them. They're as mean as a passel of riled snakes."

"And you say they're not friends of yours?"

"They're not friendly to anyone who ain't a Puma. Whenever Arvil and me came across 'em, we skedaddled the other way."

"Too bad the Utes didn't come across both of you."

"Now, now. Only a few young bucks are on the warpath and they're not about to tangle with the Pumas. There's too many of them."

"The Pumas make the Utes mad and the Utes will wipe them out."

"Nice palaver we're havin'," Eb said.

"The rifle or the pistol," Fargo prompted.

Eb shifted his weight from leg to leg and looked longingly at the Sharps and then at the revolver on his hip. "This is stupid. You shouldn't ought to point rifles at people if you don't have the gumption to squeeze the trigger." He straightened and a slow smile spread across his face. "In fact, it just hit me. If you're one of those who won't shoot an unarmed man, then you won't shoot me." He lowered his arms, and laughed. "I have you figured out."

"No," Fargo said, "you don't." He shot Eb in the leg.

Blood spurted and the mountain man pitched onto his side. Howling with pain and fury, he clamped his hands to the wound. "Damn you!" he screeched. "You had no call to do that!"

"You almost blew my head off," Fargo reminded him. "Sure I did."

Eb thrashed and clenched his jaws and hissed through his nose.

"Whenever you want to grab for a gun," Fargo said.

Shaking his head, Eb snarled, "No you don't! You're not goadin' me into it."

"I can shoot you in the other leg."

"You miserable bastard," Eb fumed. "Miserable, stinkin' no-account—"

Fargo took aim. "This next will be for all the people you've killed."

"You don't wear a badge," Eb cried. "You can't do this."

"You have it backward. If I wore a badge I couldn't. But since I don't . . ." Fargo shot him in the other leg.

The swearing and the yowling went on a long time. When at last Eb subsided, he was drenched in sweat and weakly muttering to himself.

"I didn't catch that," Fargo said.

Sucking in a deep breath, Eb spat, "When I'm healed I'm comin' after you."

Fargo went to the Sharps and picked it up and tossed it a good fifteen feet. He walked over to Eb, snatched the revolver, and threw it over next to the Sharps. Careful to keep one eye on the mountain man, he walked to the Ovaro.

"What are you up to?" Eb asked suspiciously.

"Saying good-bye."

Once on the stallion, Fargo reined up the mountain. He followed the trail, the sun warm on his face. Part of him warned that it was a mistake not to kill Eb outright. But there was a line he wouldn't cross, and one of them was shooting an unarmed man. If that brought more trouble down on his head, so be it. It separated him from the true killers like Eb and Arvil.

Fargo came to a shelf. Drawing rein, he checked his back trail. He doubted Eb would come after him, the shape Eb was in, but it didn't pay to take anything for granted. He was about to move on when he happened to glance at a ridge to the south, and swore.

Five riders were on its crest. Evidently they had heard his shots and were scouring the lower slopes. Even at that distance he could tell they weren't white. They were Utes, young Utes unless he missed his guess, and probably out for white blood. He saw one of them extend an arm in the direction of where he had left Eb, and all five goaded their ponies down the rise.

Fargo couldn't think of a more fitting end for the son of a bitch. He rode on.

It was early evening when a pinpoint of orange light drew him to his companions. They had coffee perking and were sitting by the fire, drinking.

"About time you caught up," California Jim said as Fargo brought the Ovaro to a halt. "I was starting to worry."

Sliding down, Fargo arched his back and stretched. "It might interest you to know that I saw your fire from half a mile off."

"Damn," California said. "I figured the trees would hide it."

"We should be safe enough," Coltraine said. "We haven't seen hide nor hair of another soul all day."

"I did," Fargo said, and imparted the news of the five Utes.

"Do tell," California said, and chortled. "Right about now they're likely skinning that polecat alive."

"Good riddance," Coltraine said.

Fargo rummaged in a saddlebag for his tin cup and brought it to the fire and hunkered. "I won't lose any sleep over him."

"I'd dance a jig if I had whiskey," California said.

Fargo noticed a rabbit that his friend was butchering for the supper pot. He hadn't had a bite since daylight and his stomach rumbled. "How soon until we eat?"

"Ten minutes, give or take." Setting down his cup, California resumed his work. "I was carving on this when Jon and me got to talking about the Pumas. He says he should pay them a visit alone."

"Why?"

It was Coltraine who answered. "They're my problem, not yours. I was the one who shot Chauncey. I need to settle this by myself."

"You're forgetting they tried to kill me, too," Fargo brought up.

"They only did that because you were with me."

"We'll go see them together," Fargo said.

"You're being pigheaded."

"I'm being practical," Fargo disagreed. "No one else lives as far back in the mountains as they do. If any deserters came this way, they're bound to have seen them."

"They might not be very cooperative," Coltraine observed, "with me at your side."

"I'll ask real nice," Fargo said.

California Jim cackled. "That's what I like about being your pard."

"You can count on him to be stubborn?" Coltraine asked.

"No." California held up a dripping piece of bloody rabbit meat. "I never know if I'm going to live through the day."

10

All the next morning Fargo had the feeling that someone was behind them. Three times he stopped and sought cover and waited but no one appeared.

After the third time, Coltraine shook his head and said, "I can't say much for this hunch of yours."

They continued deeper into the range, Fargo's intuition clanging like a church bell.

The afternoon dragged. They saw a few deer and spooked a cow elk.

The scenery was spectacular. Many of the peaks were over ten thousand feet, some more than eleven thousand. Broken by narrow, winding canyons and deep valleys, the range was a maze.

Here and there were verdant parks and coves that until only a few years ago had never been trod by white men.

Fargo got a crick in his neck from looking back so much.

He never spotted anyone.

Sunset found them in a broad belt of firs dappled by the spreading shadows.

"This is a good place to camp," California suggested. "It's out of the wind and our fire will be hid."

Fargo drew rein at the next clearing they came to. As soon as the fire was crackling and California was tending to their supper, he grabbed his Henry and announced he would be back in about an hour.

"You still think someone is back there?" Coltraine said.

"I do."

"Keep your eyes skinned," California cautioned. "If it's Eb, he'll be out for your blood."

Fargo moved into the timber. The shadows were spreading. His thumb on the hammer, he glided along in a preternatural twilight.

The birds were in full chorus, warbling and trilling and chirping as if serenading the setting sun.

Fargo had covered several hundred yards when he caught movement ahead. Dropping flat, he crawled to a log, took off his hat, and peered over. What he saw filled him with surprise and consternation.

Five painted Utes on horseback were tracking them.

Three had bows, one a lance, the last an old Hawken.

Behind the five, sagging in his saddle, was Eb.

Fargo didn't know what to make of it. By rights Eb should be dead. Yet apparently the mountain man had joined forces with the Utes. Even more surprisingly, Eb had his Sharps. Confident they wouldn't hear the slight click, he curled back the Henry's hammer.

The warrior with the Hawken appeared to be the leader. He raised his arm and the rest stopped. Turning, he said in fair English, "It not be long now, white-eye."

Fargo knew that some Utes spoke the white tongue. He'd befriended a Southern band a while back and gotten to know them well.

"About damn time," Eb growled. "I can't wait for you to tie that son of a bitch down so I can gut him."

"Me give word you can," the warrior said. "Me speak with straight tongue."

Eb's legs had been crudely bandaged and the bandages were stained scarlet. So were his pants. Placing a hand over the wound on his right leg, he swore and said, "I speak with a straight tongue, too. I promised you whites to kill, Two Hawks, and soon you'll have your chance."

"You strange white-eye," Two Hawks said. "You turn on own kind."

"Like hell," Eb said. "They're my enemies, the same as the Blackfeet are yours."

"They white," Two Hawks said.

"Hate is stronger than skin," Eb said, "and there's one of them I hate more than anything for doing this to me." He motioned at his legs.

"So you trade them for you," Two Owl said, not without disgust.

"I did what I had to," Eb declared. "Hell, you had a knife to my throat. I had to do something."

Fargo had it, then. Eb had bartered for his hide, offering three whites for his own life. He shared Two Hawks' disgust.

"We soon find," the Ute said. "We soon kill."

"Remember our bargain," Eb said. "I get to kill the son of a bitch called Fargo, and I get to go free after."

"Me remember," Two Hawks said.

Fargo slid the Henry across the top of the log, steadied the barrel, and fixed a bead on Eb's chest. They drew closer, and when they were twenty yards out he stroked the trigger smoothly and cleanly and had the satisfaction of seeing Eb flip backward off his saddle and tumble in a disjointed sprawl.

Jacking the lever, Fargo took aim at Two Hawks but the young Ute was too quick for him and reined into cover. The rest were doing the same. Fargo settled the front bead on a red back, only to have the back disappear.

Jamming his hat on, Fargo crawled away from the log. They'd have an idea where he was. He rounded a thicket, passed under a spruce, and rose behind an oak.

The forest was deathly still.

Eb's horse hadn't spooked and was nipping at grass near the body.

Fargo peered to one side and then the other. He had no grudge against the Utes. Were it his decision, he'd as soon let them depart unharmed.

Forty feet off, a patch of high weeds rustled ever so slightly.

To his left, the low limbs on a pine moved.

On the right, a boulder acquired a second shadow shaped nothing like the boulder.

The Utes were converging.

Fargo took a gamble. Cupping his hand to his mouth, he hollered, "Two Hawks! Can you hear me?"

The furtive movements ceased. From the high weeds came a muffled reply.

"Me hear, white-eye. What you want?"

"The man who was out to harm me is dead. We have no reason to fight."

"Plenty reason," Two Hawks shouted. "You white-skin. We red."

"I'm a friend to the Utes," Fargo tried. "I hold your people in high regard."

"Whites take land. Whites kill Utes. We kill whites."

"I'm not in your country to do your people harm," Fargo explained. "I'm here after some whites who have broken white laws."

Two Hawks was quiet a bit; then he called out. "You wear star on shirt?"

"I'm not a lawman, no. I'm a scout. I work for the army," Fargo said without thinking.

"Army?" Two Hawks repeated, and his voice had hardened. "You ride with bluecoats?"

Fargo wanted to kick himself. "Sometimes."

"Bluecoats fight for all whites," Two Hawks said. "Bluecoats have bad hearts."

"That doesn't mean I do." Fargo tried to pacify him. "I give you my word I come in peace."

No response came.

"Two Hawks? Did you hear me? I come in peace."

From a different spot came a reply tinged with scorn and distrust. "White-eye speaks with two tongues."

"What can I do to earn your trust?" Fargo tried a final time.

"You die now," Two Hawks said.

Fargo didn't waste more breath in trying to reason with them. He slipped around a pine and wove amid saplings to a boulder as high as his chest. Dropping flat at its base, he stared back the way he had come.

He didn't have long to wait. They were eager to spill his blood.

Vague shapes flitted in the darker patches. A lithe form darted from tree to tree.

Fargo aimed at a silhouette just as an arrow whizzed inches above his hat. The warrior appeared, nocking another shaft, and Fargo shot him in the head.

The woods became still again.

Crabbing backward, Fargo put the boulder between him and the warriors and rose. It was still four to one. He didn't dare stay in one spot.

Another arrow nearly caught him in the shoulder.

Fargo bolted. He ran a dozen yards, ducked behind a pine, and dipped to his knees.

None of the Utes came charging after him. They'd learned quick, these young warriors.

The forest was silent but they were out there and they were stalking him.

Fargo began to circle. If he could get behind them he'd have the edge.

The crack of a twig to the west brought Fargo up short. He didn't think any of the Utes had gone in that direction. It puzzled him until the explanation rocked him with the force of a blow. Praying he was wrong, he moved toward the sound. He'd gone maybe thirty feet when he saw them, and silently swore.

California Jim and Coltraine had heard the ruckus and were coming to his aid. They were side by side, California with his rifle at the ready, the gambler holding his twin Colts.

Fargo straightened and waved to try to get their attention. Instead he got a Ute's. An arrow thudded into an oak next to him. Ducking, he dashed in among some firs. They were spaced so close together that it would be difficult for a bowman to hit him. His intention was to run out the far side and shout a warning to his companions.

Out of nowhere, a buckskin-clad form reared and a lance was thrust at Fargo's chest. He sidestepped, let go of the Henry, and grabbed the lance to prevent the warrior from thrusting again. Before he could set himself, a moccasin swept behind his legs, and the next he knew, he was tripped and flung to the ground with the Ute on top.

Fargo drove his knee up and in. It connected but all the warrior did was grunt. Then the Ute's own knees were on his chest and the lance shaft was pressed against his throat. He pushed but the Ute was immensely strong. The lance gouged deeper, cutting off his breath.

The warrior snarled and said something in the Ute tongue that Fargo didn't catch.

Fargo struggled with all his might. His lungs urgently needed air. He bucked but the Ute stayed on him. He rammed a knee at the Ute's back but it had no effect. The warrior was determined to kill him, no matter what.

Fargo tried to roll, and couldn't. He could feel himself weakening. His chest was fit to explode. He arched his back and sought to flip the Ute off and once again failed.

In another minute he would be dead. A desperate measure was called for.

Suddenly taking his right hand from the lance, Fargo streaked it to his holster. He tried to hold the lance at bay with one hand but it felt as if his throat was being crushed. Frantic, he groped for his Colt.

It wasn't there.

It had fallen out, probably when he was tripped.

Fargo's lungs were on the verge of collapse. His head was swimming. The Ute's painted features kept blinking in and out. He had only moments to live, moments to think of something to save himself.

The Ute reared to bring more of his weight to bear on the lance and yipped in triumph.

Fargo's life was fading.

11

In desperation Fargo grasped at a straw. Bringing his right boot as close to his hip as he could, he clawed at his pant leg and raised it high enough to plunge his finger into his boot. In a twinkling he molded his fingers to the hilt of the Arkansas toothpick and slid it out. As his consciousness flickered, he stabbed the double-edged blade into the Ute's side. The warrior stiffened and gasped, and his grip weakened. Rallying, Fargo rammed the knife into him again, and yet a third time.

The young Ute let go of the lance and put a hand to his ribs and tried to stand.

With a last effort, Fargo drove the toothpick up under the warrior's sternum.

A cry was torn from the warrior's lips; not a victory cry but a death rattle. He doubled over and sank onto Fargo's chest.

So weak he was barely able to move, Fargo pushed the body off. He knew he should get up. Other Utes were still out there. But he couldn't. He was spent, his throat raw, his arms trembling slightly. Sucking in deep breaths, he sought to recover.

Shadows fell across him, and Fargo braced for the worst. He would sell his hide as dearly as he could.

"Help me get him up," California Jim said.

"I've got this side," Coltraine said.

Arms looped around Fargo and he was hauled to his feet. A hand appeared, holding his Colt.

"This was in the grass," Coltraine informed him, and shoved it into his holster.

Wetting his lips, Fargo managed to croak, "There are three more."

"We better get back to camp," California said to the gambler. "They might go for our horses."

"My rifle?" Fargo said. His head was beginning to clear and he could breathe again.

"I have it," Coltraine said.

The pair moved swiftly, bearing practically Fargo's entire weight.

After about fifty yards Fargo got his legs under him and tried to shrug them off, saying, "I can manage."

"Not fast enough you can't," California Jim said. "And if we lose our horses, we're in a world of trouble."

Fargo let them carry him almost the entire way before he gave each a push and announced, "I can do it on my own, damn it."

The woods were dark with impending night. Fargo half expected Two Hawks to utter a challenge or a threat but he didn't.

"Where did Eb get to?" California asked when the clearing came in view.

"He's dead," Fargo said.

"Shucks. I'm all broke up."

Everything was as they had left it. Their fire still crackled. Their horses were still there.

"We can't stay here," Fargo said. He was worried the remaining Utes would spring an ambush.

"Why not?" Coltraine asked.

"Do you want to take an arrow? Or be shot?"

The gambler glared at the forest. "This is why I hate the wilderness."

They didn't waste any time. Gathering up the coffeepot and their other effects, they got the hell out of there.

Fargo led. He was nearly his old self, and the ride helped to further clear his head. He went more than a mile and stumbled on a gully. It wasn't deep but it would shelter them and their animals.

Once again they set about making camp.

Fargo's first sip of coffee was a balm for his sore throat. He sat and drank and shut from his mind how close he had come to going under.

As if California were reading his thoughts, he said, "You were lucky, hoss."

"Don't I know it."

Coltraine was chewing jerky, and scowling. "I don't know as I'd call it luck that now we have three Utes on our trail instead of one mountain man."

"They might let us be," California Jim said. "It's cost them two and they don't like to throw their lives away."

"I don't think they'll give up easy," Fargo said. Two Hawks had struck him as a good hater.

"Since this business started it's been one damn thing after

60

another," Coltraine complained. "And we haven't even reached Puma Valley yet."

"You're the coon who wanted to come along," California said. 'If it were me, I'd have stayed in Hadleyville."

"You don't know the Pumas," Coltraine said. "If I don't settle with them, I'll have Pumas after me from now until the end of time."

"Settle it how? Kill Garrick Puma?"

"I'll talk to his mother."

California was about to tilt his cup, and stopped. "Do what, now?"

"It's the mother who runs things. The father was killed by a grizzly about a year ago."

"How would you know that?" Fargo asked.

"I play cards with a lot of people," Coltraine said. "I hear things."

California said, "So you'll go up to their ma and ask, pretty please, that her boys quit trying to blow holes in your noggin?"

"Something like that," Coltraine said.

"And she'll be more than happy to forgive you for killing her other son, Chauncey," California said sarcastically.

"There's that," the gambler admitted.

"You're taking an awful chance."

"I gamble for a living, remember?"

California turned. "What do you think, pard? Is this card slick asking for an early grave?"

"It's a long shot," Fargo said.

"So is a royal flush," Coltraine said.

Fargo settled back on his saddle and drank and rubbed his throat. With all the excitement he hadn't given much thought to the deserters but now he did. That there hadn't been any sign of them wasn't surprising. The Mountains of No Return covered so much territory that it was akin to searching for a needle in the proverbial haystack.

"I've had a thought," California Jim said, and he didn't sound happy about it. "What if this Two Hawks you told us about goes for help? He might ride to his village and come back with fifty warriors."

"We're in for it if he does," Fargo said. "But I suspect he'll want the credit for himself." Two Hawks had lost two men. As the leader of the war party he would be held to account for their deaths. To restore his honor in the eyes of his people, Two Hawks must slay their slayers. "We'll take turns keeping watch. I'll take the first spell."

"Like hell," California said. "You need rest. I'll go first, Jon can take the second, and you last."

Fargo didn't argue. After his ordeal he was weary to his marrow. He pulled his blanket to his chin, pulled his hat down over his eyes, and was asleep within moments. He slept so soundly that he was slow to wake. Coltraine was shaking his arm fit to break it off when he sluggishly opened his eyes and said thickly, "What?"

"Rise and shine," the gambler said. "Or at least rise." Yawning, he moved to his blankets. "Everything has been quiet so far."

Fargo grunted and sat up. He was stiff and sore and his throat hurt like hell. Thankfully, there was coffee left, and he eagerly filled his cup. It took three cups before he felt even halfway his normal self.

Tossing his blanket off, Fargo stood and shambled to the horses. The Ovaro and the others were dozing, their picket pins secure.

Fargo returned to the fire. Draping his blanket over his shoulders, he filled his cup yet again.

California was snoring and muttering. Coltraine was covered by his blanket.

In the distance to the north, a wolf howled. Closer, an owl hooted.

Fargo hadn't been paying much attention to the night sounds but now he did.

Presently, a coyote yipped. Once more the nearby owl hooted.

Fargo sat up. The owl sounded authentic and yet something about it bothered him. He waited for the cry to be repeated and when it wasn't, he told himself he was fretting over nothing.

Then the owl hooted again, east of their camp—and was answered by another owl in the woods to the west.

Fargo lowered his hand to his Colt. He was sure now. The Utes were out there. He reckoned they'd wait until first light to attack.

Time crept on claws of tension.

Fargo stayed hunched over with the blanket over his shoulders and the Colt in his lap. He put on a casual front by drinking more coffee and nibbling on jerky.

Far to the east the horizon faded to dark gray and then to light gray.

Fargo picked up a stick and poked at the fire. Holding his hand low to the ground so the Utes wouldn't notice, he also poked California Jim's boot. California snorted but didn't wake up. Fargo poked him harder.

"What the hell?" California mumbled from under his hat and his blankets.

"Stay put," Fargo whispered. "We have visitors and I don't want them to know you're awake."

"The Utes?"

"No. Little Bo Peep and her lost sheep."

"Was that a joke?"

Fargo swore. "Of course it's the Utes, you lunkhead," he whispered. "They have the clearing surrounded but there are only three of them."

"And three of us."

"Coltraine is still asleep."

"Wake him too," California urged.

"He's on the other side of the fire," Fargo whispered. "They'd see."

"How do you want to do it, hoss?" California asked.

"They'll wait for the sun to come up to be sure. Only Two Hawks has a rifle and it's a single shot."

"Arrows can kill as quick as lead."

"But they'll have to get in close so there aren't any trees or brush in the way," Fargo said. Otherwise, their arrows were easily deflected.

"If this doesn't go right we're dead."

"I like how you always look at the bright side of things," Fargo whispered as he gave the burning firewood a few more pokes.

"The bright side is that you sent two of them to their happy hunting grounds."

"I didn't want to. They didn't leave me any choice. Now hush. We've done too much talking as it is." Fargo wanted the Utes to think both the others were still asleep. "Be ready to jump up when I say to."

From across the fire Coltraine said, "Does that include me?"

"You're awake, Jon?" California Jim whispered.

"No. You're only dreaming I am," Coltraine said.

California was quiet for all of ten seconds. Then, "Why are you two picking on me?"

"Not another word," Fargo cautioned. "It could happen any minute." The faintest of pink bands rimmed the horizon.

"Now we have to fight Indians," Coltraine muttered. "The next time I get an urge to come up into these mountains, one of you should bean me with an anvil."

"I'd do it," California said, "if I could lift one."

Fargo took his eyes off the forest to say, "Clam up or you'll give us away." He looked up, and stiffened.

Two Hawks was silhouetted against the vegetation, the Hawken to his shoulder. He was taking deliberate aim—at Fargo.

12

Fargo threw himself to the left. He heard the Hawken boom but didn't feel searing pain. He tried to cast the blanket off to use his Colt but part of the blanket was caught under his legs and he couldn't.

Coltraine had no such problem. He swept out from under his blanket with both pistols blazing, triggering an ambidextrous fusillade that sent Two Hawks scurrying.

California Jim rose, too. He had his rifle up and was sighting down the barrel when an arrow struck him in the right shoulder with a *thump* and jarred him off balance. California cried out and clutched at the arrow.

Fargo finally tore his own blanket off, and rose. He fanned a swift shot at the Ute bowman just as the warrior vanished into the greenery. He couldn't tell if he scored.

"Go after them, pard," California urged. "Don't worry about me."

Fargo didn't want to. But if the Utes got away they'd likely try again. "Stay with California," he said to Coltraine, and sprinted for the spot where Two Hawks had been. Two Hawks was the key; make maggot food of him and the other two might call it quits and head for their village.

Fargo reached the trees and crouched. Right away he heard something, an odd sort of scratching and scrabbling, like a heavy object being dragged. Swaying weeds pinpointed where. He stalked over, his skin prickling at the prospect of taking an arrow or a heavy slug from the Hawken.

It was the Ute who had put an arrow into California. Fargo's shot had caught him high on the chest and he was streaming blood like a pump streamed water. He'd dropped his bow and was snaking along with effort.

"Serves you right," Fargo said.

The warrior stopped and craned his neck. His dark eyes mirrored raw hate. He said something in the Ute tongue that Fargo didn't quite hear.

"Ready to die?" Fargo said, and pointed his Colt. He was about to fire when the warrior stiffened, uttered an inarticulate screech, and collapsed.

Now there were two.

Fargo moved on.

To the east a golden glow had replaced the gray and Fargo could make out trees and boulders and a sparrow that was flitting from branch to branch.

Other birds were rousing, and avian serenades broke out all over. It was a morning ritual, the birds greeting the new day in their own fashion.

Fargo ducked under a low limb, slowly. He skirted a boulder, slowly. He'd penetrated a hundred feet or more when hooves drummed. Two Hawks and the last Ute were fleeing—or slipping away to try again another day. The sounds rapidly receded.

Fargo frowned. He'd wanted to end it then and there. Replacing the spent cartridges, he returned to the clearing.

California Jim had stripped to the waist and Coltraine was carefully digging at the arrow with a dagger.

"Skye!" California gratefully exclaimed. "How about you give this a try? Jon, here, is about as gentle as an avalanche."

"I don't have much experience at this sort of thing." Coltraine justified his awkwardness.

"And you ain't getting any with me," California said. "I swear, your poking and prodding hurts more than the damned arrow."

"See if I ever try to treat a wound of yours again," Coltraine said.

"Is that a promise?"

Fargo nipped their argument in the bud by going over and pulling his Arkansas toothpick. The arrow's barbed tip was a good two inches into California. It would have gone deeper but it struck the collarbone. "This will take some digging," he let him know.

"Not you too?" California said.

Coltraine was watching the woods. "What about the Utes? Are they still around?"

"They lit a shuck," Fargo said, slicing the tip of the toothpick under California's skin.

California winced. "You ain't much gentler than he was. More thumbs than fingers, the both of you."

"We should let him take the damn arrow out," the gambler said. "It might remind him to be more civil."

"I'll show you civil," California said, and attempted to rise.

Fargo held him down. "What are you trying to do? Bleed to death?"

"There's not that much blood."

"There will be if you don't behave."

"You're worse than my mother," California complained. "God rest her soul."

Fargo made it a habit to hone the toothpick often to keep it razor sharp. A good thing, since he had to cut deeper than he liked. Blood was oozing down California's chest. "This is going to hurt like hell. Do you want a stick to bite down on?"

"I could use a bottle," California said.

"That makes two of us," Coltraine declared.

Fargo carefully twisted and pried. The barbs were ingeniously designed so that once they were embedded, the curved tips couldn't be removed without tearing a lot of flesh.

Beads of sweat dotted California's face. "This is worse than that time I cut out an ingrown toenail with my bowie."

"Why didn't you have a sawbones do it?" Fargo asked to take his mind off the pain.

"And waste money I could spend on whiskey or a whore? Not likely."

"A man has to have his priorities," Coltraine said with a smirk.

"Exactly," California said, and abruptly sobered. "Hold on. Did you just poke fun at me?"

A golden crown lit the woodland. The stars were gone, the sky a vivid blue, a few clouds floating like islands.

Fargo pried at the tip. He was half afraid he would find it discolored from being dipped in rattlesnake venom or some other poison but it didn't appear to be tainted. He wasn't making headway and pried harder, and California Jim groaned.

"God Almighty, that hurts, pard."

"Are you sure you don't want something to bite down on?"

"Maybe I do, at that."

"I have something," Coltraine said, and went to his saddlebags. He came back with a handkerchief.

"You haven't used this to blow your nose?" California asked.

"Only once or twice," the gambler joked.

California wadded it and stuffed the wad between his upper and lower teeth and clamped down.

Fargo went on prying and working the arrow with his fingers. It was delicate work. He finally succeeded in freeing one of the tips and had to hold the arrow steady with his other hand so it didn't cause California more pain.

"This is taking forever," Coltraine said. "Can't you just rip the damn thing out?"

California's eyes widened and he said something they couldn't make out.

"What was that?" Coltraine said.

California took out the handkerchief, and spat. "You rip it out and I will by God shoot you."

Fargo said, "I almost have it." A strand of flesh was caught fast. He tried to ease it over the end of the prong but it wouldn't stretch far enough. He snipped it with a quick cut. Then, easing the arrow out, he held it for California to see. "Here you go."

"Thank God." California sank back. "I am plumb wore out."

"From a little thing like having an arrow dug out?" Coltraine said.

"I could just kick you."

Fargo wasn't done. He cleaned the wound with water and wiped it with the handkerchief. Then he held the toothpick's blade to the fire and waited for it to glow.

"What are you doing?" California asked.

"It needs to be cauterized."

"God."

"It will only hurt for a minute."

"Give me that handkerchief back." California bit down, his whole face glistening, and gulped.

"Want me to hold him down so he doesn't move?" Coltraine offered.

"Keep your eyes peeled for the Utes." Fargo shifted his grip on the toothpick's hilt as the heat from the blade grew uncomfortable.

"I'd like another shot at them," Coltraine said. "We should scalp the ones you already killed."

"No," Fargo said.

"Why not? Indians scalp whites all the time."

"Some tribes do. Some don't." Fargo didn't hold with the practice, himself. He'd heard tell it got its start among whites back before the Revolutionary War when bounties were offered for each scalp lifted. "I'm not about to."

"Why not?"

Fargo looked at him.

"I have no qualms about it. If it's good enough for the savages, it's good enough for me."

By now the toothpick was glowing red. "Here we go," Fargo said.

California clutched his saddle and his leg and grimly nodded.

Fargo pressed the flat of the blade to the wound. There was a hiss, and smoke rose, and with it the stink of burned skin.

California shook worse than ever but didn't recoil or scream.

Fargo held the blade there for a good half a minute, long enough to ensure scar tissue would form and keep it from festering or bleeding. Finally he jerked the blade away. "That should do it."

Letting out a gasp, California removed the handkerchief and went limp.

"Did he just pass out?" Coltraine asked.

"Appears so." Fargo didn't blame him. It had to have hurt like hell. He cleaned the toothpick and dried the blade on his pant leg and slid it into his ankle sheath.

Coltraine was examining California. "Say, you did right fine. You should be a sawbones. In a couple of weeks, he'll be good as new."

Refilling his cup with coffee, Fargo sat back. "I figure we'll let him rest until noon or so and be on our way."

"I hate all these delays."

Fargo was growing tired of his complaining. "You can go on ahead if you're so inclined."

Coltraine shook his head. "Don't get me wrong. I like your friend. Let him rest as long as need be." He gazed about them. "I just want this over with so I can get the hell out of these mountains."

Fargo didn't blame the gambler, either. The Mountains of No Return were living up to their reputation. "We should be near where the Pumas are supposed to hole up."

Coltraine gazed past him. "Nearer than you think."

Fargo turned.

At the edge of the clearing stood a woman in buckskins, holding a Sharps carbine on them.

13

The woman came toward them.

The first thing Fargo noticed was how attractive she was; she had a tanned oval face with red full lips and high cheeks framed by corn silk hair. She also had green eyes and a fine nose. The second thing he noticed was that her loose-fitting buckskins couldn't hide the shapely contours of her body. The third thing was the saucy sway to her hips. Giving her his friendliest smile, he said, "How do you do, ma'am."

"Don't ma'am me, mister," she returned in a throaty voice. "Who the dickens are you and what in blazes are you doin' here?"

"Utes," Fargo said. He held up the arrow and nodded at California.

She came around to where she could see the wound, and scowled. "Those damned heathens. They've given us nothin' but grief since the day we came. Were it up to me, I'd wipe out every last one of the red sons of bitches."

"Oh my," Coltrane said. He was holding his Colts at his side. "A genuine lady of the forest."

"Huh?" She looked the gambler up and down. "Listen to the fancy dude. How come you dress like a parson but you pack two pistols?"

"I'm a student of the cards, fair lady," Coltrane said, with a bow. "You could say it's in my blood."

She snorted. "I want nothin' to do with your blood." Fixing those lively eyes on Fargo, she said, "I'm Aggy Puma, by the way."

"Aggy?" Fargo said.

"Short for Agatha. I was named after my grandma. I hate it but I'd never tell my ma. It would break her heart." Aggy lowered her Sharps carbine, which was a shorter version of the rifle used by Eb and Arvil. "And you still haven't told me what you're doin' here."

"We're hunting army deserters," Fargo informed her. "Maybe you've seen them? One goes by the name of Luther Mace."

Aggy made a show of knitting her brow and pondering. "Can't

ay as I recollect the handle." She suddenly trained her carbine on Coltraine. "Suppose you put those six-guns in their holsters. You holdin' 'em makes me nervous. I don't trust you worth a lick."

"I'd never shoot a beautiful creature like yourself," the gambler said suavely.

"Did you just call me a critter?"

Fargo laughed. "You have to forgive him," he said. "He's city bred."

"I know all about his kind," Aggy said. "A tongue slick who only cares about wettin' his wick."

"I bet your pardon," Coltraine said.

"Don't play innocent," Aggy said. "I had my suspicions the moment I set eyes on you." She gestured at Fargo. "Now this pretty one here, he ain't no city boy. I know quality when I see it."

"Pretty one?" California stopped wincing and chuckled. "Like he-bears to honey, I tell you."

"Quality?" Coltraine said.

"What are they on about?" Aggy asked.

Fargo held a finger to the side of his head and moved it in a small circle.

Aggy chortled. "I can believe it with the tongue slick, there. But your other friend seems a mite country to me, even if his buckskins look fit for a squaw."

"Here now," California said.

"He's a famous scout," Fargo informed her.

"Maybe he is," Aggy said, "but he ain't nowhere near as pretty as you. And I do so like the pretties."

"If you could make it into a drink," California said to Fargo, "we'd be rich."

"Hush."

"Bottle what?" Aggy asked.

"He has this notion that ladies always take a shine to me," Fargo said.

"He's right." Aggy cradled her carbine in the crook of her elbow. "Tell you what. I better take you down to meet Ma. She'll decide what to do with you."

"I don't know as I like the sound of that," California said. "What gives her the right to decide anything?"

Aggy motioned. "This here is Puma land. We claimed it and we don't let any strangers in. There's near forty of us, so all I have to

71

do is let off a shot and you'll have my whole family breathin' dowr your necks faster than you can shake your noddle."

"Shake our what?" Coltraine said.

"God, city breds are dumb," Aggy said. "How about you get shirt on the famous scout, here, and saddle your animals and I'l take you down the mountain."

"I'd like that," Fargo said.

Aggy coughed and her cheeks tinged pink. "You must have tc beat the girls off with a stick."

California was sitting up, his hand on his wound. "My pard say no? That was a good one, gal."

"Is that how it is?" Aggy said with a mischievous grin at Fargo

"You have no idea," California said.

Fargo wasn't in any hurry. He took his time saddling the Ovarc and Jim's mount and helped Coltraine tie their packs on the pack-horse. Aggy followed him wherever he went and kept up a running account of how her family had moved to the Rockies from Tennes-see to start a new life for themselves because they were tired of being crowded.

"Why, back to Possum Hollow," she remarked, "it got so we had neighbors on all sides and not one more than four or five miles away."

"You call that crowded?" Coltraine said.

"Says the city man," Aggy retorted. "Mister, country folk live on game. And when there's that many folks, all out huntin' every day for their cookin' pots, it ain't long before the game is as scarce as hen's teeth."

"Too many mouths," Fargo said.

"Exactly." Aggy smiled sweetly. "So my pa, he got to talkin' tc the man he bought his shine from, and he heard about these Rock-ies and how in some parts there ain't a livin' white soul for a thou-sand miles or better."

"And here you are."

"You catch on quick," Aggy complimented him. "We all of us packed up and made our own wagon train. It took more than six months for us to find the spot we wanted."

"In the Mountains of No Return."

"Pa liked the name," Aggy said. "He reckoned as how it would keep others away."

"You don't find it hard to make ends meet?" Fargo inquired.

"Not when we live mainly off the land," Aggy said. "The few supplies we need, we go into Hadleyville once or twice a year."

California Jim was about to climb on his horse. Fargo went over to offer a hand but California shook his head.

"I won't be babied, thank you very much."

It took three tries but California climbed on and sat with his head bowed, holding the saddle horn. "Damn. Now I'm half dizzy."

"By tomorrow you'll be dancing a jig," Fargo said.

"I wouldn't know how."

Fargo stepped to the Ovaro and forked leather. Bending, he held out his arm to Aggy Puma. "Care to ride or would you rather walk?"

"Ride with you?" Aggy said, and girlishly giggled. "You don't have to ask twice."

Fargo swung her up behind him. "Hold on as tight as you want," he advised. "I won't break."

"That's good to hear." Aggy pressed against his back and looped her left arm around his waist. She contrived to run her palm over his midriff. "Goodness gracious, you're hard."

Fargo glanced at his crotch. "Not yet."

Aggy cackled in delight. "No, I meant you have a lot of muscle." She snuggled closer and said throatily, "This is right cozy."

"Isn't it, though?" Fargo could feel her warm breath on the nape of his neck. Down low, he stirred.

"My ma would likely say I'm actin' like a hussy but so long as a gal keeps her clothes on, I don't see the harm."

"I like how you think." Fargo clucked to the Ovaro. "You'll have to guide me."

"Head due west. You'll see for yourself soon enough."

The forest closed around them, a green shroud alive with life and sounds.

"You got a wife?" Aggy asked.

"No."

"As good-lookin' as you are?"

"I think I'd know if I had one."

"Maybe you had one in the past?"

"No."

"You ever plan to in the future?"

"No."

"I bet if the right gal came along, she could change your thinkin'."

"Hell," Fargo said.

"She could," Aggy insisted. "Ma likes to say that sooner or later every man steps his foot in the noose."

"That's as good a way to describe it as any," Fargo said.

"You have an awful low opinion of womanhood."

"I have an awful low opinion of chains."

Aggy snickered. "Listen to you. The truth is that you like to drink from the teat without havin' to buy the cow."

"There's that," Fargo said.

"At least you're honest about it. My cousin Cyrus goes on and on about how he cares for me with all his heart, and true love is true love."

"Your cousin?"

"Third removed," Aggy said. "Us Pumas like to marry among our own."

"That leaves me out," Fargo said.

"I didn't say it was ironclad or nothin'," Aggy said. "Fact is, us womenfolk take outsiders to our beds from time to time, permanent."

"The rest of the Pumas don't mind?"

"Ma says it freshens the blood, and she ought to know. She was an outsider until she was thirteen. That's when Pa and her got hitched."

"She was that old?" Fargo pretended to marvel.

"Twelve is the usual age so that's not much," Aggy said. "Look at me. I'm twenty-two and I still ain't found a man."

"You're practically an old maid."

To Fargo's amusement, Aggy drew back and sadly nodded. "That's what Ma keeps carpin' about. She says if I don't find me a man soon, I'll spend my old age alone and withered."

"Wouldn't want that," Fargo said.

"Thank you." Aggy slid forward so they were glued at his shoulder blades and her breasts. "You might ought to give it some thought."

"We've only just met."

"So? Beatin' around the bush never gets a body anywhere. You want somethin' in this world, you reach out and take it."

"Is that the Puma philosophy on life?"

"I don't know about no philosophy," Aggy said, "but our take on things is that it's us against the world. Anyone causes us trouble, we feed them to the worms."

"That's good to know," Fargo said.

14

Fifty yards of woodland brought them to the brink of a bench that overlooked a verdant valley. Bisected by a glittering blue stream, the valley was a slice of civilization in the midst of the primitive.

Fargo drew rein and said simply, "I'll be damned."

Cabins were spaced along both sides of the stream at random intervals. A few had corrals. One, and only one, had a barn.

Several vegetable patches had been planted but not a single acre had been tilled for crops. Children scampered about. Women were hanging up wash or skinning a deer or talking. Men were engaged in a variety of tasks; chopping firewood, honing a knife, wheeling a cart of hay into the barn.

"Not many folks have set eyes on our sanctuary, as Ma likes to call it," Aggy said.

"I hope she's as nice as you," California Jim said.

"Heck, I'm not nice," Aggy said. Stretching up, she whispered in Fargo's ear, "What I am is randy for a man."

"I would never have guessed," Fargo said.

"Head on down and I'll introduce you," Aggy said.

Gigging the Ovaro, Fargo noticed that Coltraine parted his frock coat so he could get at his Colts.

"Yes, sir," Aggy went on with undeniable pride, "we've carved us our own little paradise. There's more game than there ever was in Tennessee and our bellies are always full. If it weren't for the damned Utes, we'd be happy as could be."

"Have they killed any of you?" Fargo asked.

"Not yet. They tried, though. The third month we were here, they attacked us along about noon. Must have been thirty of the painted devils, whoopin' and a hollerin'." Aggy laughed. "But we gave them what for. Pa made it a rule that we're never to go anywhere without our long guns, and those heathens weren't halfway down the mountain when we peppered them with lead. We dropped three in the first rush. They tried a second time but all of us were shootin', the men and the women and some of the kids with their squirrel guns. Drove those red coyotes clean off."

"That was the last time?"

"Since then they've helped themselves to some of our horses and killed a few of our dogs and one night they shot a fire arrow onto a cabin roof."

"Your family stayed on anyway."

"We sure as hell did," Aggy declared. "We're not about to let a pack of redskins drive us off."

Fargo was surprised the Utes hadn't come back with more warriors. All the nearest band had to do was send word to other Ute villages and hundreds of painted avengers would rally to their cause. "You and your family are lucky you're still breathing."

"You'd think so, wouldn't you?" Aggy enigmatically replied.

Some of the people below had spotted them and were pointing and shouting. The news spread from cabin to cabin, and well before Fargo reached the valley floor, a considerable crowd had gathered. All the adults had guns. Even the women.

One woman, in particular, was a walking armory; she had a rifle and a brace of pistols and not one but two knives around her stout waist. She wore a muslin dress and a yellow bonnet that did little to brighten her somber features. Her eyes were pits of suspicion and intelligence. "What have we here?" she demanded as Fargo and his friends came to a stop.

"I found them up yonder, Ma," Aggy said. "That there one," and she pointed at California, "taken a Ute arrow."

The matriarch focused on Fargo. "You're a far piece from anywhere, mister."

"I'm not the only one."

"Wilma Puma is my name. We're all of us here kin."

"So I've been told," Fargo said. He scanned the half ring of faces; not one was friendly.

Wilma frowned at her daughter. "Get down off that horse, girl. You shouldn't ought to throw yourself at a man like you do."

"Oh, Ma," Aggy said. But she slid down and stepped to her mother's side.

"What are you doin' in this neck of the woods?" Wilma wanted to know.

"They're after deserters," Aggy answered before Fargo could. "Lookin' for a man called Luther Mace."

"Is that a fact," Wilma said. "Did you tell them there's no Mace here?"

"I did."

Coltraine kneed his horse up next to Fargo's and said more loudly than he needed to, "I'm not after deserters. I came to talk to the head of your clan."

Wilma tilted her head and regarded him strangely. "That would be me. What do we have to talk about?"

From the middle of the crowd a man called out, "I can answer that one."

Fargo's gut tightened.

Garrick Puma came strolling out from among his kin, his stovepipe at a jaunty angle, his hand on the pistol in his holster. Two others came with him. The same two who had been with him in town.

"Explain," Wilma said.

Garrick pointed at the gambler. "He kilt Chauncey."

"Well now," Wilma said.

"I came to explain my side," Coltraine told her, "and to settle things so there's no bad blood between us."

Garrick laughed. "Ain't he somethin'?" Another man said, "He must be loco to think we'll let him get away with it."

Wilma raised a hand. "No one does him in unless I say so," she commanded. "I reckon we can extend the courtesy of hearin' him out."

"He killed Chauncey, damn it," Garrick repeated.

"I heard you the first time," Wilma said gruffly. "And don't you be takin' that tone with me, boy, or I'll box your ears."

Fargo decided to help the gambler's cause by saying, "It's smart of you to hear him out. You wouldn't want the army coming after you."

"What do they have to do with this?" Wilma asked.

"We're working for them," Fargo said, with a nod at California. "And they know we were coming this way. Anything happens to us, they'll investigate."

"Is that so?" Wilma said, and her mouth curled in a little smile.

"Ma'am," California interjected, "if you don't mind, I'd surely like to climb down and rest. I lost a heap of blood and I can barely sit my horse."

"Where are my manners?" Wilma turned and faced her kin-folk. "Pay heed. These two are stayin' at my place." She indicated

78

Fargo and California. "They're my guests. No one is to raise a finger against them or you'll answer for it."

"What about me?" Coltraine asked.

"You can stay where you please."

Garrick Puma looked ready to explode with wrath. Wheeling, he stalked off, his companions in tow.

"Follow me," Wilma said to Fargo.

Her cabin was the one with a barn. All the dwellings were well built, the logs chinked with clay to keep out the cold wind in the frigid winters and keep in the welcome warmth from their fireplaces. All had stone chimneys. Her plot was one of the few with a vegetable garden, and a corral, besides.

"Nice place you have here," Fargo commented to get on her good side.

Wilma shrugged. "It's not all that big but it has all the comforts. You're welcome to put your animals up in the barn if you'd like. There's stalls, and grain."

"I don't see any fields of oats or wheat," Fargo said.

"We get it from town. We're hunters, not farmers."

Fargo swung down and helped ease California off his horse. "I'll take care of yours. Go rest."

"I'm obliged, pard." California was pale and slick with perspiration. "Used to be a little prick like this wouldn't affect me much."

"I'll put some coffee on," Wilma volunteered. "That'll perk you up."

Fargo and Coltraine started for the barn. Aggy wanted to tag along but her mother called and she frowned and went with Wilma and California.

A rooster and a dozen chickens pecking at the dirt parted when Fargo approached.

"What do you make of it all?" the gambler asked as they entered.

"So far so good," Fargo said.

"You don't think it strange that they live so far from anywhere?"

"Some people like to keep to themselves."

"But to set down roots in the Mountains of No Return, of all places."

"Hill folk are hill folk whether they live in the hills or the mountains," Fargo said. "They don't scare easy, and they have enough guns that they figure they can handle anything that comes their way."

"You almost sound like you admire them," Coltraine said.

"I admire grit," Fargo said. He stripped his saddle and saddle blanket and did the same with California Jim's mount and placed both in stalls. He helped himself to some oats and was about done feeding the horses when the gambler made another remark.

"That Garrick will cause trouble. I feel it in my bones. I wish I'd put lead in him back in Hadleyville."

"We're under Wilma's protection," Fargo mentioned. "That should keep him in line."

"We'll see."

The cabin had a small porch barely wide enough for a rocking chair. Wilma was in it, her rifle across her lap.

"My daughter is inside tendin' to your Jim. I had him lie down in my bed."

"He'll think you aim to marry him," Fargo said.

"Not hardly," Wilma said with a quiet laugh. "I'll never take another man to my bosom, out of respect for my Samuel."

"A grizzly, I heard," Fargo said.

Wilma nodded and her eyes moistened. "Over to the creek, it was," she said, gesturing at the stream. "He went to fetch a pail of water. Didn't take his rifle like he should have. And it was his own rule." She coughed and touched a finger to the corner of her right eye. "The griz came out of the woods and around the barn without anyone seein'. Sam was on his way back when it charged. I heard him holler and ran out to help but the bear had him in a death grip."

"I'm sorry," Fargo said.

"Sam should have taken his rifle. As for that bear, I shot it and skinned it my own self. You'll step on its hide when we go in to eat."

"I'd like to talk about me," Coltraine said.

"Would you, now," Wilma replied.

"And about Chauncey. He didn't leave me any choice. He drew on me."

"Is that your story?"

"There were witnesses, madam."

"I ain't no whore," Wilma said. "You'll address me as Mrs. Puma or call me by my given name."

"All I want to know," Coltraine said, "is that there won't be any reprisals."

"Repri-what?"

"That you won't hold his killing against me."

"Mister, you kill one of us and then you come here and ask that we forgive and forget. Is that how this goes?"

"Pretty much," Coltraine said.

Wilma Puma laughed.

15

For an hour they made small talk. Wilma was evasive about the Chauncey issue, which didn't sit well with Coltraine.

Fargo finally got around to what had brought him there. "About the deserters we're looking for—"

"I already told you we hadn't seen any," Wilma cut him off.

"There have been reports of a lot of them coming this way," Fargo patiently noted. "I'm surprised none of you have come across their sign."

"Are you callin' me a liar?"

"Why would you lie about a thing like that?" Fargo rejoined.

Wilma said indignantly, "Ours is one valley in the middle of all the mountains. These deserters of yours must go another way."

"I need to find where they get to."

"It's that important?"

"To the army it is," Fargo said.

Aggy came out and over to the rocker. "California Jim is asleep, Ma. He was feelin' awful poorly. I think he has a fever."

Fargo hoped not. Infected wounds killed more people than the guns or bows that caused them. "When he wakes up let me know."

Aggy leaned her back to the wall and secretly gave him a wag of her hips. "How about I give Mr. Fargo a tour of our valley, Ma?"

"How about you don't throw yourself at him, you little hussy."

"I am gettin' on in years," Aggy said.

Wilma looked Fargo up and down. "I suppose you could do worse. He sure is easy on the eyes."

"I'm not looking to get married," Fargo bluntly declared.

"Once a gal sets her sights on a man," Wilma said, "what the man wants don't hardly count."

"It does with me," Coltraine said.

"Was I talkin' to you?" Wilma said curtly. "My daughter knows better than to latch on to a city feller. None of you are worth a gob of spit."

"I resent that."

"Resent it all you like," Wilma said.

82

"About that tour, Ma?" Aggy prompted.

"Sure. Go ahead. I have to have a serious talk with city man, here, anyway."

Beaming with delight, Aggy grabbed Fargo's arm and practically pulled him toward the creek. "Where would you like to start?"

"It's your valley."

"I'll show you where Pa was killed."

A path had been worn from all the times the family went for water. It brought them to a gravel strip that bordered a shallow pool. The water was as clear as glass.

"Right here," Aggy said. "He'd dipped the bucket and turned to come back and the griz came over that bank and was on him before he could run. Why he didn't take his rifle I will never know."

"It only takes one mistake," Fargo said.

Aggy squatted and cupped her hand and took a sip. She wet her brow and her neck and watched a bald eagle on the wing high in the sky. "The wilds ain't for amateurs. Nature puts on a pretty face but she has fierce claws."

"I couldn't have put it better myself."

Aggy grinned. "You sure tickle my fancy. You tickle it more than anything."

"I'm not looking to get married," Fargo said again.

"Don't put the cart ahead of the horse," Aggy said. "I don't know how you are in bed yet."

"What did you mother say about throwing yourself at me?"

"She was young once. She knows you don't buy the bull until you're sure he can stud."

Fargo laughed.

"It's not funny. A girl looks for certain things in her man and that's one of the most important."

Fargo was about to say they thought alike but she might take it the wrong way. He settled for, "I like a woman who's good in bed."

"Who says it has to be in bed?" Aggy winked and took his hand in hers and strolled along the stream, humming and sashaying as if she were a lady of the night displaying her wares.

They passed several cabins, and other Pumas stared. None came near them or called out to her.

"I must have the plague," Fargo said.

"You can't hardly blame them," Aggy said. "Strangers nearly always cause trouble."

"All I'm after are the deserters."

Aggy veered toward a finger of firs that poked into the valley from above. "Come with me. I know just the spot."

"For what?"

"Where we won't be disturbed." Aggy grinned and walked faster. "I've got me an itch only you can scratch."

"You come right out with it."

"Why shouldn't I? I'm not one of those prim and proper females who only parts her legs if the man treats her like a queen."

Fargo wrestled with himself. On the one hand, she had a luscious body that he would like to caress all over. On the other, it might make Wilma mad, and he needed to stay in her good graces. "What will your mother say?"

"Who's goin' to tell her?" Aggy replied. "She'll guess, sure enough, but so long as we don't rub her nose in it, she'll let it pass."

"I hope so," Fargo said.

"Don't tell me a big, strappin' man like you is afraid of my ma?" Aggy teased.

They hadn't gone ten yards in the firs when they couldn't see the cabins, and no one could see them. Apparently Aggy had a specific spot in mind because she peered ahead and said, "It should be just up ahead."

"What should?"

Aggy pointed.

A rock outcropping jutted from the slope. Erosion had worn away the bottom, creating a pocket about six feet wide and six feet deep but only five feet high. She grinned and winked. Ducking, she slipped in and sat and patted a carpet of pine needles.

"This here is my hideaway."

Fargo took off his hat, tucked at the knees, and joined her. Once under the overhang, they were virtually invisible to the outside world. "Do you come here often?"

"As much as I can," Aggy said. "It's peaceful and quiet. If I could I'd stay the nights here but Ma would have a fit. She's a stickler for bein' in the cabin at night. Says it's a lot safer."

"With the Utes and grizzlies running around, she has a point." Fargo put his hat to one side and slid so his back was to the rock wall.

Aggy placed her rifle aside and did the same with her knife. "You haven't asked me why I brought you in here."

Fargo grinned. "You gave me a good idea. I figure you'll get round to it sooner or later."

"Sooner," Aggy said. She bent and commenced to tug at her boots. "No kissing and fondling first?"

"I told you I'm not one of those prissy city gals."

"I've met prissy country girls."

Aggy got a boot off and bent to the second. "Then I'm not prissy, period. I see somethin' I want, I go for it. I see a man I like, go for him."

"Go for a lot, do you?"

Aggy stopped tugging and said sharply, "You can go to hell is where you can go. Just because I ain't prissy don't make me that kind."

"Which?"

"You know damn well. I ain't no whore. I don't sleep with every man jack who comes along. And it's not as if I don't have the chances, neither, what with—" Aggy stopped.

"What with what?" Fargo goaded.

"Nothin'." She resumed tugging. "Damn, you chatter a lot for a fella."

"So why is it you've never married, as pretty as you are?" Fargo asked.

Aggy smiled coyly. "You think I'm pretty, do you? I thank you for the compliment."

"There's a lot about you most men would appreciate," Fargo said.

"There's a lot most men wouldn't, too. I'm headstrong, for one thing. As willful as a wild mare, is how Ma likes to put it." Aggy got the last boot off and tossed it next to her rifle. "Why are you just sittin' there? You aim to do it with your clothes on?"

"I'm keeping watch."

"Who or what is goin' to find us?" Aggy said. "Or is it you think we might have been followed?" She shook her head. "If it'll make you feel better, go have a look-see."

Fargo flattened and crawled to the opening. The firs were quiet. In the distance children were playing and laughing and somewhere a dog barked.

"You want the real reason I ain't hitched yet?" Aggy said to his back. "It's my cousins. Ain't one of them I cotton to. Not *that* way anyhow."

"Who says you have to marry a cousin?"

"Like I told you before, that's how us Pumas nearly always d
it. Since as far back as anyone can recollect."

Fargo knew that some backwoods clans were close-knit in mo
ways than one.

"I'm partial to outsiders but the ones who come by ain't fit hu
band material. They have no more backbone than a blade of grass

"What makes you say that?"

"A man with backbone would stick."

"Stick to what?"

"Anything," Aggy said evasively.

Fargo thought he spied movement below. He waited and finall
saw a large gray squirrel on the ground, its tail flicking as it darte
here and there.

"Some of my cousins have taken it personal," Aggy rambled o
"They say I think I'm too good for them. And they treat me li
dirt."

"That's not right."

"No, it sure as hell ain't. Not that I give a lick. They can go
hell. It's my heart and my body and I'll give them to who I dam
well please." Aggy paused and sorrow crept into her voice. "Pa wa
on my side. He told me not to listen to anyone who tried to mak
me do somethin' against my will." She paused again. "I miss him
I miss him an awful lot."

"What about your mother?"

"Ma sticks up for me but she doesn't understand why I've he
off. She's been on me about it more and more and I can't say as
like her naggin'."

"Stick by your guns," Fargo said.

"I intend to." Aggy gave a nervous little cough. "I reckon yo
can turn around now. And I warn you in advance. If you laugh I'
liable to grab my rifle and shoot you."

"Why would I laugh?" Fargo asked as he started to turn. He go
all the way around and barely managed to hide his surprise.

Aggy was naked.

"Why would I laugh?" Fargo said again, and then realized wh
and said, "Oh."

16

"It's another reason I ain't taken a man," Aggy said quietly. "It's downright embarrassin'. Like bein' born without a nose or ears."

"Your buckskins hide it well," he said.

"Why do you think I wear them so loose?"

The rest of her, Fargo saw, was absolutely fine. She had a flat stomach and nice hips and her thighs were exquisite. Her thatch formed a fluffy triangle at the junction. What with her tousled hair and her full red lips, she was as alluring as could be, breasts or no breasts.

"Well?" she said.

"A woman doesn't need tits to be pretty and you're as pretty as they come."

Aggy brightened. "What a sweet thing to say." She patted the ground. "Enough of this jabber. How about you come over here and prove it?"

Fargo slid next to her. "Just so we're clear," he said. "I'm not looking for a wife."

"Just so we're clear," she replied, "all I want to do is fuck."

Fargo laughed. He spread his arms and she came into them and hungrily glued her mouth to his. She kissed fiercely, passionately, as if seeking to devour him. When he parted his lips she sucked on his tongue. Her nails dug into his shoulders so hard, it hurt. Their kiss lasted a long time.

"Not bad," Aggy said huskily when she eventually drew back. "You've had practice."

Fargo flexed a shoulder. "I'm going to need salve for the scratches when you're done."

Aggy giggled. "You just might. I tend to be a she-cat and she-cats have claws."

"Claw away," Fargo said.

Aggy pressed to him again and impatiently pulled at his shirt. He helped her slide it off. She pried at his gun belt and got it off and loosened his pants. He thought she was going to strip them off but she licked her lips and plunged a hand inside.

Fargo stiffened, in more ways than one. She fondled and gripped him and smiled.

"Oh my. I got me a big 'un."

Fargo couldn't speak for the constriction in his throat.

"Cat got your tongue?" Aggy said, and laughed. "Men are all the same. A gal gets hold of their pecker and they can't hardly think straight."

Fargo covered her nipples with his palms and pinched each one.

Aggy gasped in surprise. "What are you doin'?" she demanded. "I ain't got no titties."

Fargo pinched each nipple again, harder.

"Oh, God," Aggy said. "Men don't hardly pay them any mind." She swooped her lips to his and delved her tongue deep into his mouth. Meanwhile, her hand stroked his pole and her fingers rimmed the tip.

It was all Fargo could do not to explode. He lowered her onto her back, none too gently. She liked it rough. The rougher, the better. When he twisted a nipple she thrust her pelvis against his and softly cried out.

"Yes! Oh yes!"

Fargo ran his other hand down over her belly to her bush and along her left thigh to her knee. Her skin was silken smooth and hot against his.

"I want you so damn much," Aggy breathed. As if to prove her point, she sank her teeth into his shoulder.

Fargo almost cried out. She bit so deep, she drew drops of blood. Her fingernails raked his back while her knee rose up and down along his inner thighs, exciting him further. She was a firebrand, this country girl.

"More," Aggy said. "More!"

Cupping her bottom, Fargo dug his own nails into her ass. She squirmed and panted and gripped his hair, practically tearing it out by the roots.

"Damn," Fargo said.

Aggy grinned in devilish lust and renewed her assault on his body. "You're so hard," she exclaimed.

Fargo didn't know if she meant his pole or his muscles. Parting her legs, he placed his palm over her nether mount.

"At last!" Aggy closed her eyes and exhaled through her nose. "Do me, handsome," she begged. "Do me until you break me."

Fargo had never heard it expressed quite that way. He did his best to oblige. Aligning his member, he rubbed it up and down her slit.

"Come on. Come on," she urged. "Put that tree of yours inside of me."

Holding himself still for a moment, Fargo gripped her hips and looked into her eyes and said, "You want it, you got it." And with that, he rammed up into her as if trying to split her in half.

Aggy came up off the ground. Her head fell back and her mouth went slack and her eyes mirrored pure raw pleasure. "Yes!" she husked. "Oh, God in heaven and Jesus, too, yes, yes, yes."

Holding on to her hips, Fargo rammed into her. Each thrust impaled her to her core. Her velvet walls clung to him, and she became as wet as the stream. He let go of her right hip to slide his hand between them and his finger found her tiny knob and circled it.

Aggy's red lips parted in a soundless scream. Her eyes rolled and the tip of her tongue poked from her mouth and she ground her bottom in wild abandon. "I'm there," she mewed, and gushed.

Her release incited Fargo to new heights. He settled into a rhythm, pacing himself, savoring the sensations and determined to make them last as long as they could.

Looking up at him in wonder, Aggy said dreamily, "You're the best ever. The very best."

"Shut up and fuck," Fargo said.

She was all too happy to comply. Their mouths met, their bodies twisted and bucked.

Fargo rocked on his knees, up and in, up and in. He went faster, ever faster, and harder, ever harder, until finally no amount of self-control could stem the inevitable. He crashed over the brink and the world burst and she cried out and clung to him.

Afterward, she lay with her head on his shoulder and curled his hair with her fingers.

"That was awful nice."

"Uh-huh." Fargo was feeling drowsy.

"Thank you for pinchin' my titties. Most men can't be bothered because they're so puny."

"Titties are titties," Fargo said.

Aggy laughed and snuggled her cheek into the hollow of his arm. "I wish more men were like you."

Fargo closed his eyes. It wouldn't take much for him to drift off.

"I wish they were as big as you, too. You're a stallion in your pants."

"You can hush up now," Fargo said.

"No, I can't. I like to talk, after," Aggy said. "Sometimes I'll talk a fella's ears off."

"Hell."

"Now, now. A gal gives herself to you, the least you can do is listen to her prattle."

"You wouldn't happen to have a candle, would you?"

Aggy raised her head. "A candle? What on earth for?" Her eyebrows pinched, and she chuckled. "Oh. I savvy. So you can peel off the wax and stuff it in your ears." She smacked him.

"You're terrible."

"I can be," Fargo said.

"Listen," Aggy said, settling back down, "I shouldn't ought to tell you this but I like you. This deserter business? You might want to go on back to the fort and tell whoever is in charge that you couldn't find them."

"I gave my word I would, and I will."

"There's been a lot of them. How do you expect to find them all?"

Resisting his lethargy, Fargo cracked an eyelid. "How would you know how many desertions there have been?"

Aggy shrugged. "People talk. Gossip and such."

"Which people?"

Placing her chin on his chest, Aggy looked him in the eyes. "Damn it. I give you advice and you give me a hard time."

"The desertions are costing the army a lot of money. They want them stopped."

"I reckon they would. But it's their own fault for offerin' so much bonus for a soldier to sign up."

"You know about that, too?"

"It's common knowledge. Why are you makin' more out of what I say than there is?"

Fargo had been thinking and now he said, "Your family must know these mountains well."

"Like the backs of our hands," Aggy boasted.

"The army thinks the deserters are passing through to the west. Maybe to Salt Lake City. From there they can scatter to the four winds and never be found."

"That sounds logical," Aggy said.

"Which trail are they likely to take? The easiest on their horses? The one with the most water?"

"There are several that run clear through."

"The closest to Hadleyville," Fargo amended.

Aggy raised her chin and scratched it. "I reckon that would be the one they call the old Bridger Trail."

"I was thinking the same thing."

"It's about five miles south of here, as the crow flies. We hardly ever use it, ourselves."

"I might go have a look at it tomorrow."

"How come you didn't straight off? What brought you to our neck of the woods?"

"I came as a favor to Coltraine," Fargo said.

"Oh. Him."

Fargo tilted his head to see her better. "You don't sound as if you like him much."

"He's too full of himself," Aggy said.

"How would you know that?" Fargo had the impression they'd never met before.

"A body hears things."

"You hear a lot."

Aggy frowned, then sat up and brushed pine needles from her arms. "You're spoilin' it. I wanted to lie here with you a spell but you had to bring up the deserters and the like."

"I was only asking."

"Well, don't."

"I'm in no hurry to go anywhere." Fargo patted his chest. "Lie back down."

"I'm not in the mood now, consarn you." Aggy grabbed her buckskin pants.

"You're prickly, is what you are."

Lifting her bottom to slide her pants up over it, Aggy said regretfully, "What I really am is too nice. My ma is always tellin' me that. She says I care for folks when I shouldn't."

"Do you mean me?"

"You shouldn't have come here, handsome," Aggy said.

"So you keep saying."

"For a good reason," Aggy said. "Because it could be you won't make it out of these mountains alive."

17

"Your friend is in a poor way," Wilma Puma announced the moment Fargo entered her cabin. "I've sent for our healer to have a look at him."

Fargo went into the bedroom.

California Jim was bundled to his chin. He was awake, and staring glumly at the ceiling. "Howdy, pard." He quaked slightly. "Reckon as how you were wrong about that arrow. It was tainted."

Fargo put his hand to his friend's brow and was startled. Jim was burning up. "I don't understand it," he admitted. He would have sworn the arrow's tip hadn't been dipped in poison.

"Mrs. Puma says she sent for someone."

Fargo debated taking California back to Hadleyville for the doctor to have a look at him. It would take several days of hard riding, and by then Jim might be a lot worse.

"Don't look so worried. I'll shake this off. You'll see."

There was a loud knock on the front door, and voices, and in a few moments Wilma came in trailed by a sprightly older man who wore clothes that had been cobbled together from odd bits and pieces of hide. Some still had hair on them. He also wore a buck-skin band to contain his long gray hair. He was carrying a black bag such as physicians used, only his was as old or older than he was, and had cracks and a few small holes in it.

"I don't rightly know as I should help heal an outsider, Wilma," the man was saying. "Your husband, God rest his soul, had a rule against it."

"He's passed to his reward and I'm the head of this family now," Wilma said. "You'll do as I damn well say."

The healer moved to the bed and placed his palm on California Jim's brow as Fargo had done, and blurted, "Land sakes. He's on fire. This ain't a good sign."

Fargo glared.

Clearing her throat, Wilma said, "Mr. Fargo, I'd like you to meet Royal Puma."

"Royal?" Fargo said.

"I hated the name when I was a sprout," the healer remarked as he groped under the quilt and brought out California's arm. "But I got fonder of it as I got older. Has a nice sound, don't you think?"

"You any good at what you do?" Fargo bluntly asked.

It was Wilma who answered. "I'll have you know that Royal has been our healer goin' on forty-five years. He hardly ever loses a patient."

Royal had hold of California's wrist and was feeling for a pulse. "She tells me you took a Ute arrow, mister."

"I did," California Jim said.

"I'd guess you have poison in your blood," Royal said. "How much and what kind is anyone's guess. But don't you fret. We'll sweat it out of you. And I've got herbs that will help."

"I'm grateful," California said, and did more quaking.

"What can I do?" Fargo asked.

"Pick daisies for all I care," Royal said. "I don't like bein' insulted."

"And I don't like losing friends."

Royal looked across the bed. "Was that a threat?"

Fargo smiled.

"Stop that, you two," Wilma said. "Fargo, he'll do the best he can. You have my word. And Royal, keep in mind these men work for the army and if one of them dies in our care, we'll have blue bellies out here sniffin' around."

"We sure enough don't want that," Royal declared.

"You don't like soldiers?" Fargo asked.

The healer answered while opening his black bag. "We don't like outsiders, period. We especially don't like those as work for the government."

"Amen to that," Wilma said. "They're busybodies, the whole bunch. They take away our freedom and call it law."

"You're free to live where you want," Fargo said. "To do what you want."

"Are we?" Royal said as he took out an old stethoscope. "Go east of the Mississippi and try to wear a sidearm in public. Or spit tobacco on a city street. Or get drunk and indulge in a jollification. The law will be down on you before you can blink."

Fargo didn't dispute the healer's point. He'd been back East a few times. Civilization, in his estimation, was a big word for treating people like sheep.

"It's part of why we came out here," Wilma said. "So we don't have to live under anyone's thumb. That includes the government's."

Royal nodded. "I'll be damned if anyone is goin' to tell me what I can or can't do."

"About my friend," Fargo said to get him back to what mattered.

"I need to examine him. Why don't you go do somethin' and not stand there distractin' me."

Fargo looked at California, who weakly grinned and nodded.

"I'll be all right, pard."

Reluctantly, Fargo went out.

Wilma followed him and went over to the stove. "Would you care for some coffee? I have a pot on."

Fargo nodded.

Going to the cupboard, Wilma took a cup from a peg.

She moved to the stove, filled it, and returned to the cupboard and took down a tin.

"What's that?" Fargo asked.

"Sugar. Or do you like yours black?"

"A little won't hurt."

Wilma opened a drawer and found a small spoon. Taking the lid off the tin, she scooped a heaping spoonful and held it over the cup. Then, with an odd sort of shrug, she upended the spoon and stirred. "Here you go," she said, bringing the cup over.

Fargo sipped. It was hot, and sweet.

"How do you like it? My Sam used to take his with enough sugar to gag a horse. He said it made his coffee as sweet as me."

"Oh, Ma," Aggy said.

Fargo took another sip, and frowned. It was too sweet to suit him. He set the cup on the counter.

"You don't like it?" Wilma asked.

"Not that much sugar," Fargo told her.

"How about I pour you another and we add just a pinch this time?" Wilma offered.

"No, thanks." Fargo had something else on his mind. "Where did Coltraine get to?"

"Your cardsharp friend and me had us a long talk," Wilma said, "and he went for a walk." She smiled. "Are you sure about the coffee? It won't take but a few seconds."

"No." Fargo went outside. He hadn't seen any sign of Coltraine on his way back from the woods with Aggy, and he wondered where the gambler could have gotten to. He gazed up the valley and down the valley and saw only Pumas. Puzzled, he walked toward the barn.

The door was open, and out of it strolled Garrick Puma, shadowed by his two cousins.

Garrick smirked and hooked his thumbs in his gun belt and said, "Well, look who it is, boys. The high and mighty scout himself."

"Have you seen Coltraine?" Fargo asked.

"Maybe I have and maybe I ain't," Garrick said, and his shadows chuckled.

"Where?"

"I sure as hell ain't about to tell you where he is," Garrick said in contempt.

"Not even if I say pretty please?"

"Not even if you get down on your knees."

"I have a better way to persuade you," Fargo said, and slugged him on the jaw.

The blow rocked Garrick onto his boot heels and his stovepipe hat went flying. Tottering, he tried to recover his balance, and failed.

His cousins were momentarily rooted in surprise. Then one squawked and both rounded on Fargo and brought up their fists.

Fargo unleashed an uppercut on the man on his right, spun, and buried his fist in the belly of the one on his left. Both crumbled.

Garrick swore luridly and pushed to his knees. "We'll pound you senseless!" he roared.

Fargo kicked him in the chest.

The Puma on the left was clawing for his Smith & Wesson, the one on the right was rising.

Fargo kicked the one and punched the other. He would have liked to pound all three into the dirt but instead he drew his Colt and trained it on Garrick. At the click of the hammer all three froze. "Pretty please," he said.

"I still won't tell you," Garrick fumed.

Someone else came out of the barn: Jon Coltraine. "What the hell is this?"

Garrick spat blood and snarled, "He attacked us without cause."

"I had plenty of cause," Fargo said, watching that none of them tried to jerk a pistol.

"Name one thing," Garrick said.

"You have bad manners."

"What?"

"And you're dumb as a stump."

Garrick wasn't amused. "You hear this?" he said to Coltraine. "You hear how funny he thinks he is? All you outsiders are the same."

"I wish you hadn't done this," the gambler said to Fargo. "It will make things worse."

"Yes, sir," Garrick said, snatching his stovepipe hat from the ground. "There are limits and this was it." He pushed to his feet and rubbed his jaw. "You hear me?"

"I hear you," Coltraine said.

The two cousins rose, the one holding his gut. "We ain't lettin' this pass," said the other.

All three wheeled and stalked toward the cabin, casting glances over their shoulders that would shatter a rock.

"You've made enemies," Coltraine observed.

"They already were," Fargo said. "And you seem to be forgetting they tried to kill us back in Hadleyville."

"I haven't forgotten anything, I'll have you know."

Fargo nodded at the barn. "What were you doing in there, anyway?"

Coltraine sighed. "Trying to persuade Garrick that I had no choice with Chauncey. It was him or me." He stared after them. "I'd about convinced him to let it drop and then you go and do this."

"Next time it won't be my fists," Fargo said.

Coltraine arched an eyebrow. "I thought you wanted their cooperation in finding Luther Mace and those other deserters?"

"I can do it without them."

"Is it me or are you testy?"

The question gave Fargo pause. He did feel irritable. Unusually so. He also felt warm and sweaty. Letting down the Colt's hammer, he shoved it into his holster. "As soon as California is up to it, we're taking the Bridger Trail to the west side of the range."

"I'm going to have a talk with Wilma," Coltraine said. "Maybe she can keep Garrick under control." He moved toward the cabin.

Fargo made for the stalls to check on the Ovaro and their other animals. He was perspiring as if it were a hundred and ten degrees. Mopping his brow with his sleeve, he hoped he wasn't coming down with something.

The horses were fine.

Fargo was patting the Ovaro's neck and the stallion was nuzzling him when a lithe form brazenly brushed her hip against his.

"Miss me?" Aggy said.

"Your brother kept me company," Fargo said sourly.

"I just heard," Aggy said. "I can't leave you alone for two seconds, can I?"

"You heard how?"

"Garrick is in there now bellyachin' to Ma about how you beat on them and how she should let him splatter your brains all over creation. You should hear him, the big baby."

"You're not on his side?"

"I know how he is," Aggy said. "He likes to lord it over folks. It gives him a feelin' of power over them."

"The prick," Fargo said.

"Ain't he, though." Aggy giggled.

"Your mother has more sense than to listen to him," Fargo predicted.

"That she does, yes, but it's not her you have to—" Aggy caught herself.

"What were you about to say?"

"Nothin' important," Aggy said.

"Don't lie to me. I thought we were friends."

Aggy scowled and poked at the ground with a toe. "All I'll say is that if I were you, I'd watch my back real careful."

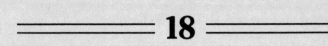

18

The next morning California Jim was worse.

Jim's skin burned to Fargo's touch. Jim's buckskins were soaked and so was the bedding but Royal Puma insisted the best remedy to deal with the poison was to sweat it out of him.

"Give it another day," the healer advised, "and your pard will be on the mend."

The last thing Fargo wanted was to stick around. Word of his fight with Garrick had spread and nearly every last Puma would dearly love to take a club to him. He saw it in their eyes and on their faces.

Wilma didn't seem to hold it against him, though.

Nor did Aggy, who agreed to watch over California Jim until he got back.

"Are you takin' your poker-playin' friend along?" she asked as he was throwing his saddle on the Ovaro.

"No." Fargo hadn't seen much of Coltraine since the fight.

The gambler hadn't spent the night at Wilma's but had shown up early that morning to let Fargo know that he was safe and staying at another cabin down the valley.

It was a little past nine when Fargo started for the Bridger Trail. He wasn't in any hurry. It was only five miles there and back. He'd be at Wilma's well before sunset.

The mountains were magnificent. The towering peaks, a few sprinkled white, the thick troves of timber, the upland parks—the Wasatch Range was a wonderland of natural beauty and wildlife.

Fargo was in his element. As much as he liked a good card game and a bottle of whiskey, to say nothing of a willing dove, he could abide only so much town life before he longed for wide-open spaces.

In one respect, at least, he was a lot like the Pumas. He relished being free to go wherever the wind blew him. He could no more adapt to city life than a wolf could adapt to living in a sheep pen.

The Bridger Trail wasn't well used. Fargo doubted more than a hundred whites a year traversed its length. The Utes used it, too, but how regularly, it was impossible to say. He would have to search to find it.

A switchback brought him to a meadow. He skirted it, and it was well he did, for as he neared the other side he spied thin gray ribbons rising from the woods.

Instantly reining into the forest, Fargo alighted and shucked his Henry from the scabbard. After wrapping the reins around a limb, he crept forward. Presently he smelled the smoke, and something else: blood.

Dropping onto his belly, Fargo snaked along until he heard voices. Exercising stealth, he was soon close enough to see the fire and its makers.

A Ute hunting party had brought down a cow elk. An elk was too heavy to be thrown over a horse or dragged on a travois, so they'd removed the hide and were butchering the meat for transport to their village.

Fargo counted seven warriors. They were talking and joking and relaxed. He also counted eleven horses and assumed the four extras were pack animals.

Turning, Fargo was about to sneak away when a twig cracked. It came from his left. Freezing, he spotted a pair of legs off through the undergrowth.

It was another Ute, returning from God knew where. He'd pass within a few yards of where Fargo lay.

Flattening, Fargo hugged the ground.

The Ute called out to the warriors at the fire and one of them answered. Apparently the warrior had gone after another elk but the elk got away.

The man's legs were almost on top of him. Any moment, Fargo expected the warrior to see him and shout a warning.

He heard the scrape of each sole and the crunch of a fallen leaf.

Then the warrior had gone by and he could breathe again.

Five minutes of crawling, and Fargo was back in the saddle. He gave the hunting party a wide berth. Another mile or so, and he came over a ridge and there was the Bridger Trail.

A novice from the East would have been hard pressed to tell it was there. It wasn't worn by wagon-wheel ruts or pockmarked with hoofprints.

Only an experienced eye could detect the serpentine break in the symmetry of the forest.

Fargo followed the trail for more than half a mile and drew rein in consternation. The only tracks were those of unshod horses belonging to a party of Utes. There was no evidence that whites had used the trail in weeks. Granted, it was remote, and granted it was hard to find, but it was the logical route for the deserters to take.

Where, then, Fargo pondered, had they gotten to? If they hadn't gone west they must have gone south or north, but either way took them deep into mountain fastnesses that few if any whites ever set eyes on.

Fargo mulled it over the whole ride back. His arrival drew stares from the Pumas, which he ignored. At Wilma's he went to the corral and was climbing down when feet pattered and Aggy rushed up.

"Thank God you're back! We've been awful worried he'd be gone by the time you got here."

"Gone where?" Fargo said.

"Not where but who," Aggy set him straight. "It's your friend, California. He's taken a turn for the worse."

Fargo ran to the cabin. He was bothered to see Garrick at the table but he ignored him and rushed into the bedroom. Wilma was standing at the foot of the bed with her arms crossed and concern on her face. Royal Puma was pulling the quilt up to California's chin.

"There you are. He's been askin' about you."

Fargo shouldered the healer aside and grasped Jim's hand. "Can you hear me?"

California's eyes fluttered open. "Pard?" he croaked. "I'm feelin' right poorly."

Fargo touched his forehead, and grimaced. California's fever was higher than ever. "I thought you knew how to heal," he snapped at Royal.

"I'm doin' the best I can, mister," the gray-haired man said. "But poison is hard to treat. I tried my remedy for snake venom, thinkin' they might have dipped it in rattler poison, but it didn't help any."

"I'm afraid he doesn't have much time left," Wilma said.

Fargo could have slugged her. His glare was enough to cause her to look hurt and leave the bedroom. He glared at the healer, instead. "What needs to be done?"

"I still think it's best to try and sweat the poison out of him," Royal said. "We keep him covered like this, and get a lot of liquids into him, it could turn him around."

California coughed. "I'm sorry to delay things like this, pard."

"To hell with that," Fargo said. "Getting you better is what counts."

"Why, Skye Fargo," California Jim said with a grin, "I do believe you care."

"You need anything, anything at all, give a yell." Fargo went out.

Garrick was gone and Aggy was at the table, staring blankly at a wall.

"Care for some coffee?" Wilma asked from over at the stove. "I have a fresh batch ready."

"Black this time," Fargo said.

"However you like."

Fargo sat across from Aggy. "Has Coltraine been around since I left?"

"He sure hasn't," Aggy replied. "Leastways, I ain't seen him, but I haven't been here the whole time."

"Your gambler friend came by earlier," Wilma informed them. "He looked in on California and said to tell you he'd be back."

Fargo couldn't fathom what the gambler was up to. The whole family held Chauncey's death against him; Coltraine was asking for a bullet or a blade in the back. "He should stay closer to your cabin."

Wilma took the coffeepot to the counter. "You're thinkin' my kin are liable to do him in?" She shook her head. "Not without my say-so they won't."

"Not even Garrick?"

"My son is a hothead, I'll grant you," Wilma said as she poured. "But he wouldn't dare go against my wishes or against what's best for the rest of us."

Fargo drummed his fingers on the table. He wanted out of the cabin. A confined feeling had come over him, and he'd like some fresh air. But she came over and set an old china cup in front of him.

"Here you go."

Fargo sipped. It was piping hot. He blew on it and took several more light swallows and noticed a slightly bitter taste that he hadn't noticed when it was sickly sweet with sugar. "What do you put in this?"

Wilma smiled and said, "You told me no sugar or cream so I left it black." She carried the pot to the stove. "I ground the beans myself. They're a mite old but they still make good coffee."

Fargo supposed that could have something to do with the bitter taste. He took another sip and set the cup down. "I'll be back in a bit," he announced, rising.

"Where are you goin'?" Wilma asked. "I thought you'd stick here because of your friend."

"I need to see to my horse."

The afternoon sun was warm on Fargo's face as he crossed to the corral. He was bending to the cinch when a sudden cramp in his gut caused him to suck in his breath. He put his hand to his stomach and leaned against the corral rails. A second cramp, more severe than the first, doubled him over. For a few seconds his vision swam and he became almost unbearably hot. "What the hell?"

"Are you all right?" Unnoticed, Aggy had joined him. "What's with your belly?"

Fargo hadn't eaten all day but that never bothered him. "It must be your mother's damn old coffee." Then he remembered. He'd felt flushed and ill for a little bit after the last cup of coffee, too.

"It should pass," Aggy said.

A third stab of pain made Fargo grit his teeth to keep from crying out. He breathed in through his nose and gripped a rail until his knuckles were white.

Aggy was studying him anxiously. "It's a good thing you didn't drink all of it, then, huh?"

Fargo grunted. A troubling thought had occurred to him, and he sorted through his recollection of events since they arrived.

"I never drink Ma's coffee," Aggy babbled on. "Everyone knows she can't make it worth a hoot. I reckon I should have warned you."

Fargo let go of the rail and willed his legs to move.

"Where are you goin'?" Aggy asked in alarm.

Fargo didn't answer. He concentrated on the stream and only the stream. Sweat poured from every pore. His legs were weak and he stumbled twice but he made it. Kneeling, he took off his hat and dipped his mouth to the water and gulped. He drank and he drank. The urge to retch came over him, and he turned and vomited. Not much, but enough that when he was done and had wiped his mouth with his hand and straightened, he was feeling more like his usual self.

"Are you all right?" Aggy asked. "Want me to fetch Royal to tend you?"

"No."

"Is there anythin' I can get you?"

Fargo stared at the cabin and the smoke curling from the chimney and thought about California Jim and raw fury coursed through him. "I could use a brain," he said.

19

The more Fargo thought about it, the more his suspicion grew. And he thought about it a lot as he stripped the Ovaro and ushered the stallion into the corral and went back into the cabin.

Wilma and Royal were at the table with cups and saucers in front of them.

Fargo made it a point to see that they were drinking tea. Grabbing an empty chair, he began to drag it toward the bedroom.

"What are you doin'?" Wilma asked.

"I'll be with Jim," Fargo said. He lifted the chair and carried it in. California was asleep.

Fargo went to a corner where he could watch the bed and the doorway, both. He turned the chair and straddled it and leaned the Henry against the wall next to him.

It wasn't half a minute before Royal Puma entered. He put a hand on California's brow and commented offhandedly, "There's no need for you to stay with him. I'll be here for as long as need be."

"So will I," Fargo said.

Royal smiled. "However you see fit." He adjusted the quilt and went back out.

Fargo bet himself a dollar that Wilma would come in next, and he was right. She entered carrying a tray with a steaming cup on it. "What's that?"

"Some tea for your friend," she replied.

"No."

"I beg your pardon?"

"No tea right now. He's sleeping."

"But it's good for him," Wilma said. "It has herbs in it. And it's hot so it will help him sweat."

"No, I said."

Wilma hesitated. "I suppose it can wait until he wakes up."

"No tea. No coffee, either," Fargo told her. "When he wakes up I want a pitcher or a bucket so I can bring him water from the stream."

"But that won't help him any."

"From here on out," Fargo said, "I say what he drinks and eats. No one else."

"What's gotten into you?" Wilma asked.

"Royal hasn't helped much," Fargo said evasively. "He told me so himself."

"Yes, but . . ."

"No buts," Fargo said. "I'll take over from here. You can rest and take it easy."

Wilma frowned. "I'm tryin' my best to be hospitable. I don't know what else I can do."

"You've done more than enough," Fargo said. He almost shot her then and there.

"Give a holler if you want anything." Wilma smiled and retreated into the main room.

Folding his arms across the top of the chair, Fargo got a grip on his temper. If time proved him right, then there would be hell to pay.

Subdued voices suggested a heated discussion was underway.

The next to appear was Aggy.

"Can I get you somethin'?"

"I'm fine," Fargo said. He was unsure how much of a part she had in it and decided to test her. "You might try some of your mother's special tea. You look a little tired."

She looked at him. "What's so special about it? Tea is tea."

"If you say so."

"I ain't much of a tea drinker, anyway," Aggy said. "Coffee, neither. Cow's milk, yes. And cold water I like a whole lot."

"I don't suppose there's any whiskey anywhere?" Fargo brought up.

Aggy glanced at the doorway and lowered her voice. "As a matter of fact, Pa kept a bottle hid out in the woodshed. I promised him I'd never tell Ma. She'd of walloped him if she'd found out."

"Is it still there?"

"I believe so, yes. If you want, I can sneak it in to you later."

"I'd be grateful," Fargo said.

Her grin was lecherous. "*How* grateful?"

"Hussy." Fargo grinned.

Aggy giggled and left.

Fargo relaxed. There was nothing else he could do short of saddling the horses and throwing California Jim over his mount and leaving, and Jim was in no condition to ride. They had to stay despite the danger. "A hell of a note," he said.

A lot of time passed. Twice Fargo felt himself dozing off. He'd catch himself, sit up, and shake his head to stay awake.

The light in the window was fading when boots thumped and Jonathan Coltraine filled the doorway. "I hear you're playing mother hen."

"I've known California a good many years," Fargo said.

"Poor Wilma is taking it personal," Coltraine said. "She thinks you think she's a poor nurse."

"Sounds like the two of you are on good terms."

Coltraine stepped to the window and parted the curtain. "We've agreed to a truce, if that's what you mean."

"She's forgiven you for killing her son? That's what I call turning the other cheek."

The gambler glanced over. "She's a smart gal. She doesn't let her emotions run away with her and always does what's best for her clan."

"When are you heading back to Hadleyville?"

"I thought I'd stick around a while yet," Coltraine said. "Help you look after Jim."

"I don't need help."

"You really are a mother hen," Coltraine said. He opened his frock coat and placed his hands on his Colts. "Well, if there's nothing I can do here, I might as well go back to Martha's."

"Who?"

"Oh. Didn't I tell you? Martha lost her husband to consumption about a year ago. She's been to town a few times and we struck up an acquaintance."

"It's good to have acquaintances," Fargo said.

Coltraine pursed his lips. "How about you? When are you going out after those deserters?"

"When he's up and around," Fargo said, with a nod at California.

"That could be a while. I can watch over him if you have a lot of riding to do."

"Martha would get lonely."

"Is it me or are you as prickly as a riled porcupine?" Coltraine said.

"Blame it on Wilma's coffee. It didn't agree with me."

"Ah," was all Coltraine said. He moved to the doorway. "I'll be back to see how you are getting on."

"You do that." Left alone, Fargo did more pondering. He ended up more puzzled than anything. Pieces of the jigsaw were missing. The why of it, for one thing.

Outside, the sun had set and twilight was spreading.

Fargo got up and lit a lamp on the dresser and placed it on a small table beside the bed. He didn't hear Aggy come in.

"Ma is fixin' stew for supper. How about I bring you a bowl when it's ready?"

"Considerate of you," Fargo said.

Aggy winked. "Selfish of me. I want you to keep your strength up for later."

"What do you have in mind?"

"As if you don't know." Aggy gave a saucy shake of her backside and sashayed out.

California Jim rolled from his back onto his side and mustered a feeble grin. "That gal sure has taken a shine to you."

Fargo hadn't realized he was awake. He sat on the edge of the bed and placed his palm on California's brow. It was warm but not hot. "How do you feel?"

"Like I was caught in a buffalo stampede and stomped half to death." California grimaced. "My damn gut is the worst."

"Cramps?" Fargo said.

"How did you know? Or have you taken a poison arrow your own self and survived?"

"From here on out you're not to drink anything but water, and only if I bring it. Do you hear me?"

"What about the tea Mrs. Puma makes?"

"Not one damn sip."

"I don't savvy," California admitted.

"Just do as I say. It's for your own good." Fargo mulled whether to reveal his suspicion and instead said, "There's more going on than we thought. I don't have all the answers yet but you're not to trust anyone except me. You savvy that much?"

California nodded.

Rising, Fargo strode into the main room.

Wilma, Royal, and Coltraine were huddled at the table, talking in low tones. Wilma saw him first, and gave a mild start. She whispered something and the others straightened and looked over.

"How's he doing?" Coltraine asked.

"I thought you'd left," Fargo said, moving to the cupboard. He opened both doors.

Wilma guessed his intent. "We use a bucket," she said. "It's out front."

Fargo stepped to the door. "I'll be back in a minute. No one is to disturb Jim while I'm gone."

"I can't even look in on him?" Wilma asked.

Royal said, "He's my patient. I need to check on him from time to time."

"When I say no one," Fargo said, "I mean no one."

"You're actin' awful peculiar," Wilma mentioned.

"It's that coffee of yours," Fargo said, and had the satisfaction of seeing her blanch. He went out. Night had fallen. The bucket was where she said it would be. Hastening to the stream, he lowered it in the water.

Windows glowed in most of the cabins, and somewhere a mother was yelling for her children to come indoors or have their backsides tanned.

When the bucket was full, Fargo hefted it and started back.

Aggy came out of the barn. "Hold on there, handsome."

"Can't," Fargo said.

In a burst of speed Aggy was next to him and matched his stride. "I only wanted to ask if we could get together later."

"What did you have in mind?"

"Don't play games. Can we or can't we?"

"I don't like leaving California alone."

"It wouldn't have to be for long," Aggy said. "We can do it after everyone else has gone to bed."

"I don't know," Fargo said.

"I'm like a bitch in heat," Aggy said. Smiling seductively, she brushed his thigh. "I'd make it worth your while."

"You're not only a hussy," Fargo said, "you're a horny hussy."

"You didn't like the first time?"

"I liked it a lot."

"Me too. And I'd like a second helpin'."

"When?"

Aggy glanced at the cabin to be sure no one was listening. "How does midnight sound? You can fuck me quick-like and then go back in with your friend. Yes or no?"

"Hell," Fargo said.

20

Aggy was true to her word. By the clock on the dresser it was a few minutes shy of midnight when Fargo heard light tapping on the bedroom window.

California Jim was asleep.

Fargo rose quietly from the chair and went to the window and parted the curtains.

Awash in starlight, Abby grinned and beckoned.

Fargo held up a finger for her to wait. Taking the chair, he wedged it against the bedroom door latch so no one could enter without making a god-awful amount of noise.

The window creaked slightly as he opened it. Easing his right leg over the sill and then his left, he slid out.

Aggy immediately molded her body to his. Kissing his cheek, she ran a finger along his jaw. "I've been dreamin' of havin' you all day."

"Keep your voice down," Fargo whispered, with a glance in at Jim.

"Sure," Aggy whispered, and kissed his other cheek. "How is he doin'?"

"A lot better," Fargo said. He almost added, "now that I'm not letting him drink anything except what I give him."

"I should tell you," Aggy confided, "Ma isn't too happy about you shuttin' her out. Nor Royal. They say they can't understand what you're up to."

Fargo looked into her eyes, trying to tell if she knew the terrible truth. "I noticed that your mother and Coltraine were getting along today."

"Why does that surprise you?"

"He killed her son. Your brother."

"Oh. That." Aggy averted her face. "Why are we talkin' about this? I came to make love, not hear about Chauncey overusteppin' himself."

"Overstepping how?"

"He should have left well enough alone. He—" Aggy stopped.

"Damnation. Listen to me. I do tend to run off at the mouth sometimes."

"I'd like to hear more."

Aggy stepped back. "Well, you're not goin' to. Either we do it or we don't. I won't be badgered with questions that I'm not allowed to answer."

Fargo was learning a lot, despite her. "Tell me one more thing and then I'm all yours."

Pouting, Aggy wriggled her foot. "I'll answer if I can but I'm not makin' any promises."

"The curtains in the bedroom look store-bought."

Aggy snorted. "*That's* what you want to know about? I reckon they are. So?"

"And there's a new clock on the dresser."

"So?"

"And the coffeepot looks new, too."

"I say again, so?"

"So you wear buckskins and Royal wears hides but a lot of other Pumas I've seen had on store-bought clothes, and not old clothes, either."

"You have eyes like a hawk," Aggy said. "But what the blazes do our clothes matter?"

"Store-bought costs money," Fargo said. "It makes more sense for your family to wear homespun."

"Spoken like a man. Let's have the womenfolk work with a needle and thread all damn day," Aggy said. "Are you ever goin' to get to the point to this?"

"Garrick's hat is new. His clothes, and the clothes his cousins wear, are new. The saddle I saw out in the barn is new. Hell, so is the pitchfork."

"You're borin' me," Aggy said.

"Where did the money come from?"

"How would I know? Ask Ma. She handles ours. Now either we get to it or you can go back in."

"I'm done," Fargo said. He glanced in at California, grasped Aggy's hand, and led her to a large oak. Walking around it, he pressed her against the trunk.

"Here?" she said. "It's awful close to the cabin. Someone might hear."

"I won't scream if you don't." Fargo kissed her ear and nipped the lobe.

"I'm serious. My ma hears us, she'll be madder than a wet hen."

"I doubt she thinks you're a virgin." Fargo went to kiss her neck but she angrily pushed him away.

"What did you go and say a thing like that for? No, she knows I'm not, but you shouldn't ought to bring it up."

"Calm down." Fargo tried to put his hand on her arm but she swatted it aside.

"You owe me an apology."

"I what?"

"When you called me a hussy, I figured you were joshin'. But now you went and said it for real, and that hurts. I'd like you to say you're sorry."

"You're being silly."

"Isn't that what hussies do?" Aggy shot back. "Say it or you can go play with yourself for all I care."

Fargo sighed. He had half a mind to say she could take her temperamental outburst and shove it up her backside but he responded with, "If it will make you feel better, I don't think you're a hussy."

"I didn't hear a sorry in there."

Suddenly reaching around behind her, Fargo grabbed the twin half-moons of her bottom and pulled her roughly against him. "Sorry as hell," he growled.

Aggy grinned. "That's better."

Fargo cupped her chin and pressed his mouth to hers. She parted her lips and hungrily devoured his tongue, her own swirling around and around. Her hand, meanwhile, tugged at his shirt, then slid up and under to caress and fondle his washboard stomach.

"Nice," Aggy cooed with her eyes closed when the kiss ended. "Very nice."

"You talk too much." Fargo licked her throat and the side of her neck and her ear. She wriggled and rubbed a leg against his.

Fargo was growing hot again, for a whole different reason.

He thrust his hand between her thighs and covered her nether mound.

"Oh!" Aggy moaned.

Undoing her buckskin britches, Fargo let them slide down

around her knees. Once again he thrust his hand between her thighs, and this time ran a finger along her slit.

Shivering, Aggy dug her nails into his shoulders. "That feels good."

"How about this?" Fargo said, and parting her nether lips, he penetrated her with his middle fingers. She moaned, and her forehead fell to his chest.

Around them the valley was peaceful. Gusts of wind rustled the higher branches of the oak and off a ways a dog howled at the crescent moon.

Fargo looked around the tree at the cabin. The only light was in the bedroom.

"Are you payin' attention or have you lost interest?" Aggy asked.

Instead of replying, Fargo slid his other hand up and under her shirt. At his first tweak of a nipple she canted her head to the heavens, her luscious lips apart. He pinched the other nipple and she bit him.

For a while their mouths and their fingers met and explored. Aggy began to pant. She tore at his pants. When they were down around his knees, she fastened her mouth to his manhood.

Unprepared, Fargo fought to stay in control. When she licked from his groin to his navel, he scooped her into his arms and lowered her to the grass. She helped him tear off her clothes. Then, eagerly spreading her legs, she grinned up at him.

"Put that redwood in me, handsome."

She was wet and yielding. Once he was all the way in, he held still, savoring the moment.

Not Aggy. She thrust and ground her hips in increasing urgency. She wanted it. She wanted it bad.

The night and the valley blurred. It was as if Fargo was in a tunnel, and at the end of it was Aggy and nothing else. His body was a piston. In and out, in and out, again and again and again, until she let out a soft cry and clung to him and spurted with a violence that swept his own pleasure to new heights.

Then it was Fargo's turn. He'd been with a lot of women but something about Aggy and the danger made his release so intense, it permeated to his marrow. He came and he came.

Drained, he collapsed on top of her. She didn't push him off as some women would do but held him and planted a multitude of tiny kisses on his face and throat and shoulders.

"Thank you, thank you, thank you."

Fargo eased onto his side and closed his eyes. He would have liked to lie there a while, floating on the ebb tides of release, but Aggy poked him in the ribs.

"Don't fall asleep, consarn you. Ma might decide to use the outhouse instead of the chamber pot and see you lyin' there."

Fargo roused and sat up. "I could have gone my whole life without hearing about your mother and the outhouse."

Aggy giggled.

Pulling himself together, Fargo adjusted his gun belt, made sure the Colt was snug in its holster, and rose. The breeze felt cooler than before.

Far off up the mountains a wolf howled.

Standing, Aggy hugged him. "I'll sneak around to the front. Ma is in my room and I'm sleepin' on blankets near the stove. She'll never know I was out." Aggy pecked him and smiled and ran off.

Fargo went around the oak toward the window. He was thinking about how Aggy was a wildcat at lovemaking, and that she had no reason to be bothered by her lack of tits. Belatedly, he sensed someone behind him, and then registered the rush of feet and the swish of the high grass. He tried to turn and a battering ram caught him between the shoulders. He was knocked to his hands and knees so hard that the world swam, and before he could recover, hands seized both of his arms and he was roughly hauled to his feet and held in grips of iron.

The face that came into focus sneered with malicious glee. "We've got you now, you son of a bitch."

"Garrick," Fargo found his voice.

"And Lester and Puce," Garrick said, with a nod at his cousins. "I've been keepin' an eye on the place, hopin' to catch you unawares. And now, thanks to my sis, I did."

"She knew you were out here?"

"Hell no," Garrick said. "She'd be mad if I told her I wanted to stomp you into the ground. She's too nice, is her problem. She's so nice, Ma won't let her in on all of it."

"All of what?"

Garrick poked him in the chest. "Forget that. I owe you for hittin' me, remember?"

Fargo tried to jerk his head aside but he was too slow. The blow rocked him. His head sagged and Puce and Lester had to firm their holds to keep him from falling.

"How'd you like that little tap?" Garrick taunted. He grabbed Fargo's shirt and shook him. "Don't black out on me, you hear? There's a lot more to come."

"Just do it," Lester said. "We make too much noise, your ma might hear."

"I ain't afraid of her," Garrick said.

"What about the other one?" Puce said.

"All right, all right." Garrick brought his face close to Fargo's. "By the time I'm done, you'll wish you'd never been born."

21

Fury coursed through Fargo. It cleared his head and pumped new strength into his sinews. With a savage oath he rammed his forehead into Garrick Puma's face—into Garrick's nose. There was a *crunch*, and wet drops splattered him, and Garrick cried out and staggered back.

"You bastard," Lester hissed, cocking his fist.

Twisting, Fargo brought his boot down with all his force on Lester's foot. Lester went rigid with pain and his mouth gaped but he had the presence of mind not to scream. Puce threw an arm around Fargo's neck but Fargo ignored it and kicked Lester where it hurt a man the most.

Lester's hold slackened, and Fargo tore his arm free. Whipping down, he flipped Puce over his shoulders. Before Puce could scramble upright, Fargo punched him in the face, once, twice, three times.

Puce was down.

Lester had doubled over, his hands over his crotch. He looked up as Fargo came at him and couldn't duck the uppercut that snapped him onto the tips of his toes and sent him reeling and falling.

Lester was down.

Fargo spun.

Garrick had drawn his knife. Blood dribbling from his ruined nose, he snarled, "I'm goin' to gut you, you son of a bitch." He spat blood, and attacked.

Backpedaling, Fargo avoided several cuts and slashes. He deliberately threw himself onto his back and brought his knees to his chest as if to drive both feet at Garrick, who retreated a step. It brought Fargo's boot close to his hand and in a heartbeat he'd palmed his Arkansas toothpick.

Garrick tried to close and Fargo kicked at him, forcing him back. Heaving into a crouch, Fargo said, "Come and get some, boy."

Garrick spat more blood, and did. His blade was longer and he was quick but not as quick.

Steel rang on steel.

Fargo pivoted, feinted, lanced the toothpick into Garrick's shoulder. Garrick squealed and skipped away, blood spurting from the wound. Fargo went after him.

Garrick ran. He bolted like a frightened deer, glancing back in fear that he might be pursued.

But Fargo didn't go on. He ran to the bedroom window and quickly climbed in. He had a fear of his own—that while he'd dallied with Aggy, Garrick and his cousins had paid California Jim a visit. To his deep relief, California was peacefully sleeping, his chest rising and falling in gentle rhythm.

Fargo opened a dresser drawer and found a neatly folded chemise. Taking it out, he used it to wipe the blood from his toothpick. He slid the knife into his ankle sheath and put the chemise back in the drawer.

Fargo stood a moment, staring at his friend and then at the bedroom door with the chair propped against it. He came to a decision. Going to the bed, he sat on the edge and lightly shook California Jim's shoulder. California mumbled but didn't wake up. Fargo shook him again.

California's eyelids fluttered and he smacked his lips and said, "Not now, Cybil. I'm too tired."

"Cybil?" Fargo grinned and poked his ribs.

Jim's eyes snapped open. "What is it, pard? What's going on?"

"How do you feel?"

California seemed to reach inside himself. "Better than I have since I took that arrow."

Fargo felt his forehead. The fever was gone. It confirmed his hunch. "It wasn't the arrow."

"How's that again?"

"Keep your voice down," Fargo cautioned. He lowered his.

"It wasn't the arrow. They poisoned you. They tried to poison me but I didn't drink enough."

California levered onto his elbows with his back to the headboard. "By they you mean the Pumas?"

"Wilma," Fargo said. "With help from their healer."

"Son of a bitch. But why murder us? It's Coltraine who killed Chauncey. What did we do to them that they want us dead?"

Fargo glanced at the bedroom door. He thought he'd heard a sound. "We'll talk about it after we get the hell out of here."

"We're leaving?"

"Just about everyone in this valley is our enemy. We stay, we're asking for a grave."

"And here I took a liking to that Wilma. She was sweet as could be."

Fargo considered his own liking for Aggy. "There's no one we can trust, except maybe the girl." He gripped the quilt and threw it off. "Need help?"

California Jim placed his hands flat and slowly sat all the way up. He swung his legs over the side, and grinned. "I'm a turtle but I can do it." He started to rise, and stopped. "Wait. What about Coltraine? He's coming with us, ain't he?"

"He's staying at a different cabin."

"We have to fetch him, then," California said. "They must want him dead even more than us, him shooting Chauncey and all."

"You'd think so, wouldn't you?"

"Where will we head after we get him?"

"Anywhere." Fargo hadn't thought that far ahead. "Hurry now." He went to the window and peered out. Puce and Lester lay where they had fallen and there was no sign of Garrick. When he turned, California was standing and gripping the headboard to keep from falling.

"I'm a mite woozy. Sorry."

"It'll pass."

"My six-gun and my rifle. Any idea where they are?"

Fargo did, in fact. He sank to a knee and reached under the bed. "I put them here for safe keeping."

"Then I'm as ready as I'll ever be."

Fargo moved to the door. He quietly slid the chair aside and opened the door wide enough to poke his head out. The room was dark but he could make out Aggy, stretched on her side near the stove. The door to the other bedroom, where Wilma was sleeping, was wide-open.

Fargo shut the door and crept to his friend. "We're going out the window."

"I sure could use something to drink," California said. "And I'm starved, besides."

"Once we're clear of the valley," Fargo promised. Reclaiming the Henry, he went around the bed and looked out the window again.

Puce and Lester weren't there.

Fargo stuck his head out and looked both ways. They were gone. Quickly sliding out, he scanned the dark as he gave California a hand down.

"I can't get over them trying to poison us. What the hell is going on?"

"Later," Fargo said. He moved to the corner.

The shroud of night mantled the valley, unrelieved by a single light anywhere. The pale glow of the stars and the crescent moon were all they had to see by but it was enough to distinguish the horses dozing in the corral, and that the barn door was open.

"Stay close," Fargo whispered.

"Like a tick," California Jim said.

Fargo was all too aware that Garrick and his cousins might be out there somewhere, watching and waiting their chance.

He moved as quickly as California's condition allowed. At the corral he handed the Henry to him and went about throwing their saddle blankets and saddles on the Ovaro and California's horse. Sliding their bridles on, he led the animals out.

"I thought I saw something, pard."

"Where?"

California Jim pointed. "Yonder. It was there and it was gone. I couldn't tell if it was a man or an animal."

Fargo took the Henry and gave him his reins. "Do you need help climbing on?"

"I have some dignity left." California slid his rifle into the saddle scabbard, gripped the saddle horn, and hooked his boot in the stirrup. With a grunt and an oath, he managed to fork leather.

Fargo swung up. Reining to the south, he gigged the stallion into a fast walk. He thought there would be shouts and shots but the night stayed serene.

"God, it's great to be out of that bed," California said. "I sweat so much, I about stunk myself to death."

Fargo looked at him.

"What?"

A dog yapped far off. It was barking at something else, not at them.

Fargo was a bundle of tension until they reached the woods.

He went a short way and realized they were following a gully that wound up toward the heights, a stroke of luck in that it hid them from searching eyes. He climbed about a hundred yards and drew rein. "This will do."

California Jim brought his horse alongside the Ovaro. "We haven't gone nearly far enough."

"We'll rest and head out at first light."

"You're doing this on account of me, aren't you? Because I've been so sickly."

"It's risky to ride at night," Fargo said. Which was true as far as it went. In the dark, low limbs and other obstacles were harder to spot.

"I won't be pampered."

"Climb down, you contrary mule." Fargo dismounted and moved to a flat area.

Grumbling, California Jim followed his example. Suddenly he tripped, and cursed.

"See? You're not yourself yet," Fargo said.

"Myself, hell. There's some kind of bump here." California shuffled a few steps, and plopped down. "How can I be so tired, all the sleeping I've been doing?"

"Try and get some sleep," Fargo advised. "I'll keep watch."

"Not all night you won't. It's only fair I take a turn, too."

"I'll wake you in two hours," Fargo lied.

"You wouldn't be trying to trick me, would you?"

"You should know me better than that." Fargo sat where he could see down the gully and placed the Henry across his legs. It wasn't long before he heard California snore, and smiled.

For a while all was peaceful, and then the distant roar of a grizzly shattered the mountains. It was a reminder, as if any were needed, that the meat-eaters were abroad. From dusk until dawn they prowled after prey in a nightly orgy of bloodletting and feeding punctuated by snarls and howls and shrieks.

Stifling a yawn, Fargo stretched. He could use some sleep but California needed it more. They had hard riding to do in the morning.

Fargo intended to return to Fort Barker. California could visit the infirmary and he'd report to Colonel Williams that the deserters had vanished into thin air.

The night proved uneventful. Once a twig snapped close by and another time a large animal rustled the undergrowth.

Faint light was breaking to the east when Fargo stirred and stood. He turned to wake California and nearly tripped over a low dirt mound about six feet long. "What the hell?" he said, remembering that California had done the same thing. He looked about them, and his skin crawled.

Dirt mounds were everywhere.

22

It took a few moments for Fargo to absorb what he was seeing. There were more than a score, some fairly recent judging from the appearance of the dirt, and others older. A few were a lot older.

Kneeling next to the one he had tripped over, Fargo began digging with his hands. It was one of the recent mounds and the dirt came away easily. He'd gone down barely six inches when his fingers brushed cloth. Scooping more earth away, he stared at a patch of blue. He dug and brushed faster, exposing more, until finally he sat back on his heels, and swore.

California Jim rolled over and opened his eyes. Blinking and yawning, he sat up. "Hell in a basket. It's almost dawn. You didn't wake me like you promised."

"You needed the sleep."

California rubbed his chin and his chest, and froze.

"What's that there you're doing?"

"Look around you."

"What in tarnation?" California said as he swiveled his head. "Are they what I think they are?"

"They are if you think they're graves."

Pushing to his feet, California turned in a circle. "Good God. I make it to be twenty-three."

"You can count without taking your boots off?"

"Hardy-har," California said, and snapped his fingers. "Wait a minute. Didn't Colonel Williams tell us there have been twenty-four desertions?"

"He did."

"And there are twenty-three graves."

"There are."

"So twenty-four minus the one you shot in Hadleyville makes twenty-three." California turned in another circle. "These must be the rest of the deserters."

"Let's find out." Fargo moved to a second mound and scraped at it with a flat rock. In no time he uncovered another blue uniform.

California was digging at yet another. Shortly he declared, "Yep.

A soldier-boy, like those two." He plopped down and shook his head. "The Pumas must have killed every damn one of them."

"That would be my guess."

"Why? What brought them here?"

"Why do you think?"

"I don't—" California gaped at the mounds and his eyes widened. "They were killed for however much money they had on them. That's why the Pumas have been so damn unfriendly and tried to murder us."

"The nail on the head," Fargo said.

"It's all making sense. Why, they're a nest of sidewinders, plain and simple."

"We have to get word to Colonel Williams." Fargo pushed off his knees and moved to the Ovaro. As he was climbing on he gazed down the gully and caught movement at the tree line. "They're after us."

"Already? The sun ain't hardly up yet."

"They can't risk us bringing the army down on their heads."

A loud howl wavered on the wind.

"Dogs!" California exclaimed. "The bastards have set their hounds on us!" He dashed to his horse. "We have to light a shuck."

"Calm down."

California uttered a harsh laugh. "Calm, he says. With an entire clan out to do to us as they did to the soldier-boys."

Fargo headed up the gully. They had a lead but it wasn't much. He needed to widen it. Accordingly, when the slope briefly leveled, he stopped and swung down.

California drew rein, too. "Why are we stopping?"

"You're going on," Fargo said as he yanked the Henry from its scabbard.

"The hell you say. I'm in this with you." California went to swing his leg over but Fargo reached out and grabbed his ankle. "Let go of me."

"You're not up to a hard ride just yet. I'll hold them here while you skedaddle and I'll catch up to you by nightfall."

"No."

"I wasn't asking."

"Damn it, pard. They poisoned me. I want them to pay. I want them to suffer like I suffered."

"I don't blame you," Fargo said, "but now's not the time or the place." He moved behind California's roan. "Head south. Don't worry about marking your trail. I'll find you."

California opened his mouth to argue, and Fargo smacked the roan on the rump.

California looked back glowering as the roan trotted off, but he didn't draw rein. Within moments he was lost around a bend.

Fargo crabbed to the edge of the slope leading down. The Pumas weren't in sight but by the sound of the hounds they soon would be. Lying on his belly, he wedged the Henry's stock to his shoulder.

The baying grew louder. The dogs were the first to appear, four of them straining at the long leashes held by their handler.

Fargo didn't recognize the Puma who held them but he did the three riders who came next: Garrick, Puce, and Lester. More followed. Six, seven, eight, heavily armed, all on horseback except the man with the dogs.

Fargo fixed a bead on the lead hound. It was only doing what it had been trained to do but he couldn't afford to be sentimental.

Unexpectedly, Garrick hollered something and the whole party came to a halt. The man holding the leashes commanded the hounds to sit. Some of the men climbed down but most stayed in their saddles.

They were allowing the dogs a brief rest, Fargo realized. He raised the sights from the hound to Garrick Puma. Taking a deep breath, he shouted, "Go back down!"

Puce and Lester and the rest on horseback jerked their rifles up. Those on the ground crouched and raised theirs. Only the man with the leashes, and Garrick, didn't show surprise.

Leaning on his saddle horn, Garrick calmly smiled and called out, "That you, Fargo? What did you say? I didn't quite hear."

"Go back down," Fargo repeated. "You get this one chance and this one chance only."

"Listen to you," Garrick said, and laughed. "You reckon you can stop all of us? Just the two of you?"

Fargo didn't answer.

"How about you, California?" Garrick shouted. "Are you as dumb as he is?" Garrick tilted his head as if anticipating a reply, and when none was forthcoming, he yelled, "It's just you, Fargo, is that it?"

"I'm enough," Fargo said.

"You had him go on ahead while you stay and delay us?" Garrick shook his head in amusement. "Noble as hell, ain't you?"

"Tell me something," Fargo hollered. "When did you start killing deserters?"

"We saw that you uncovered some of the bodies," Garrick replied. "Who told you they were there?"

"No one."

"Liar. You didn't just stumble on them. I bet it was my idiot sister."

"She had no part in this," Fargo said.

"You got that right," Garrick said. "She's too tenderhearted for her own good. She knew some deserters came here but Ma said we had to keep the actual killin's from her."

"You did it for the money."

"That, and the fun."

Fargo was sorely tempted to squeeze the trigger. "You think it's fun to kill?"

"Don't you?" Garrick hollered.

"How is it they all wound up in your valley?" Fargo fished for more information.

"Wouldn't you like to know."

"You lured them here somehow," Fargo speculated, "or tricked them."

"We are tricky devils," Garrick said, and he and several of the others cackled.

"Did you spread the word in Hadleyville that your family would give deserters a warm welcome? So they'll come here thinking they can hide out for a while and instead you buck them out in gore and take all their money?"

"Not Hadleyville," Garrick said.

"Where else?"

Now it was Garrick who didn't answer.

"Was it your brainstorm or someone else's?" Fargo continued to stall.

"Much as I'd like to, I can't claim credit," Garrick said, and added sarcastically, "The big brain did it."

"Your mother?"

"Ma is smart but she'd never come up with a marvel like this in a million years."

Fargo was about to probe further when Puce Puma said something to Garrick, who nodded and rose in his stirrups.

"You've kept us here long enough, don't you think?"

"You're not getting past me," Fargo vowed.

"Tough talk. It's time to test your mettle and see if you're half the hard case you pretend to be."

"One last question," Fargo yelled.

"Make it quick."

"How good a shot are you?"

Garrick seemed surprised at being asked. "Damn good, I'll have you know."

"Yet you fired all those shots at Coltraine and me in town and didn't hit either one of us."

"It wasn't for lack of tryin'."

"Then you're not as good as you claim."

"It was dark and you two were runnin' around like rabbits," Garrick said. "What does it matter, anyhow?"

"I'm just trying to get it clear in my head."

Garrick bent toward the man with the dogs and spoke and the man nodded. When Garrick straightened, he was grinning. "You poked fun at my shootin'. We're about to find out how good you are."

"There will be blood," Fargo warned.

"I'm countin' on it." Garrick raised his arm but paused as someone came up the gully and called to him.

It was Aggy. Ignoring the other men, she stalked to Garrick's animal. "What's the meanin' of this? I saw all of you ride off with the dogs and came to find out what you're up to."

"Go back down to Ma," Garrick said.

"I will not. I demand an answer. Who you are after? Fargo and California?"

Garrick motioned at two men who climbed down and attempted to take her by the arms.

"No, you don't," Aggy said, leaping back and leveling her Sharps carbine. "Anyone lays a finger on me will regret it."

"Damn it, sis," Garrick said.

"Damn yourself."

Garrick turned to the dog handler. "We have no time for this, Clevis. Let the hounds loose and we can plant him with the others."

"Plant who?" Aggy said.

The man called Clevis slipped the leashes from the big hounds, pointed up the gully toward Fargo, and yelled, "Kill him, you hear? Kill! Kill! Kill!"

23

The four hounds bayed fiercely as they bounded up the gully.

Fargo didn't have time to run to the Ovaro and get out of there. He had no doubt the dogs had been trained to rip their quarry to pieces, and he'd be damned if he'd let that happen. Centering the Henry's sights, he squeezed off a shot.

With a startled yip, the lead hound pitched onto its face and rolled to a limp stop.

The other three kept on coming.

Fargo worked the lever, aimed, fired.

A second hound crashed down.

Jacking in another round, Fargo sighted and smoothly stroked the trigger.

Scarlet sprayed from the third beast's neck and it sprawled and thrashed.

The last dog came to a sudden stop. It looked back at its fallen fellows and displayed a remarkable sense of self-preservation; it fled into the forest.

The Pumas didn't waste another moment. At a bellow from Garrick, they charged Fargo's vantage point.

Fargo coolly worked the lever yet again. They'd just made their worst mistake. The Henry held fifteen cartridges in its tube magazine and another in the chamber. That made sixteen shots, and he'd used only three. He had thirteen left.

There were twelve Pumas.

Puce and Lester were out in front, yipping like Comanches. The rest came after them. Several banged off shots that buzzed over Fargo's head.

"You asked for this, you sons of bitches," Fargo said as he sent a slug into Puce Puma's chest. He shot Lester, then a third man. He shot a fourth, a fifth, a sixth.

Only then, with their ranks so drastically thinned, did the other Pumas come to a bewildered stop. They looked at one another and at the dead and they did as the last hound had done. With jabs of their spurs and lashing their reins, they scattered right and left into the woods.

Fargo let them go. He could have shot a few more but he had a few scruples and one of them was that he didn't shoot people in the back, if he could help it. The crash and crackle of the vegetation assured him they were fleeing and weren't circling to get behind him.

Rising, Fargo scanned the slope to be certain all those who were down would stay down. Not one so much as twitched. Going to the Ovaro, he opened his saddlebags and took out a box of Henry cartridges. It didn't use the same ammunition as his Colt. Squatting, he set the box on the ground and opened it. One by one he fed cartridges into the tube. He'd finished and was about to close the box and rise when a metallic *click* behind him turned him to stone.

"I can't tell you how much I want to kill you," Garrick Puma said.

Fargo looked over his shoulder.

Garrick held a six-shooter level at his hip. His face was lit with a nearly maniacal lust to kill. "Drop the goddamn Henry."

Fargo let the rifle fall. He didn't see any other Pumas. "You're alone?"

Garrick swore. "Those yellowbelly cousins of mine. Lit out like a bunch of spooked does. But not me. I snuck on up here, figurin' to catch you off guard. And look at you, at my mercy."

Fargo's right hand was close to his right thigh, below his holster. He could draw but not before Garrick put a slug into him.

"You massacred us," Garrick growled.

"The same as you massacred the deserters," Fargo said to keep him talking.

"Like hell," Garrick said. "We did them a few at a time. The most was the three we killed last."

"Did you feed them first and act like you were their friends?"

Garrick laughed a cold laugh. "They came here thinkin' we'd help them escape by leadin' them across the mountains."

"I wonder where they got that idea," Fargo said.

"You'll never know."

Fargo moved ever so slightly. "Where did your sister get to? I lost sight of her."

"Aggy?" Garrick said, and blinked. "I forgot about her. Where *did* she get to, I wonder?"

"Right here," Aggy said as she came out of the trees with her Sharps carbine at her side.

"Damn it, sis," Garrick said. "Go on home like I told you to."

"All this time you've lied to me. You and Ma, both."

"You would have raised a fuss," Garrick said. "Now do as I say and go."

Aggy bobbed her chin toward Fargo. "I like him, Garrick. I like him a lot."

"You don't listen worth spit."

"I don't want you to kill him," Aggy said.

Garrick became livid with anger and took his eyes off Fargo to glare at her. "Will you listen to yourself? He just shot six of your kin."

"They were tryin' to kill him."

"Have you any brains at all? He was sent by the army to track down the deserters. What do you reckon the army will do if he goes back and tells them about the graves he found?"

"How did they die, Garrick? All those soldiers?"

Garrick clamped his mouth shut.

"Did you shoot them or stab them?"

"Neither," Garrick spat.

"I've had an awful suspicion for a while now," Aggy said. "I didn't want to admit it could be true. Not about you. Not about my own ma. But whenever some of them showed up, Ma would invite them in and feed them. And I'd never see them again."

"Everythin' we did, we did for the family."

"How did killin' all those men do us any good?"

"Where do you think we got the money for all the new things we've bought? That chamber pot you like? That dress you never wear?"

"Ma said it was money Pa had squirreled away."

"Pa was dirt poor. He never had a spare dollar his whole life long. And Ma and me got tired of it. A lot of the others were tired of it, too."

"So you killed all those soldiers for their money?"

"And their horses and their saddles and their guns and whatever else we could sell. We have a man on the west range who buys it all."

"I thought I knew you. I thought I knew Ma."

"Don't you look down your nose at us."

"How about if I do?" Fargo said, and when Garrick glanced at

128

him, he drew. He fired as Garrick tried to turn, fired as Garrick tried to raise his six-gun, fired as Garrick's knees buckled. His ears ringing from the shots, he barely heard the thud of the body.

Aggy came over. She stood above her twitching brother and tears trickled down her cheeks. "God help me," she said softly. "I reckoned if I kept him talkin' it would give you a chance."

Fargo rose and placed his arm around her. "For what it's worth, if you ever need a friend, you send word and I'll come as fast as I can."

Aggy looked him in the eyes and heaved a long sigh. "I wish it was more than that." She sniffled, and began to cry.

Fargo pulled her to his chest and she buried her face and gave vent to her sorrow. Only when she had cried herself out did he step back and say, "This isn't over yet. You know that, don't you?"

"Must you?" she asked in a little voice.

"They have to answer for it, the same as him," Fargo said, nodding at Garrick.

"They won't let you leave the valley alive."

Up the gully hooves drummed, and around the bend came California Jim. When he stopped he stared at Garrick and down the slope at the dead men and the dead dogs and said, "Good God Almighty."

"You were supposed to be a long way off by now," Fargo said.

"I couldn't run out on you, pard," California said. "Not when I heard all those shots."

"It's just as well." Fargo commenced to reload. "Look after her while I go end this."

"You're going back?" California patted his revolver. "I'm going with you."

"No," Fargo said, "you're not." He picked up the Henry, brushed it off, and slid it into the scabbard. Stepping into the stirrup, he mounted and lifted the reins. "Go about a mile and make camp. If I don't show up by nightfall, in the morning head for Fort Barker."

"Be careful," Aggy said.

Fargo clucked to the Ovaro. He threaded through the bodies and brought the Ovaro to a trot and didn't slow until he came to the graves. Shucking the Henry, he approached the tree line with caution. He couldn't predict how many he'd have to go up against. Maybe only those with Garrick were a party to the murders. Aggy probably wasn't the only one who had been kept in the dark.

For the middle of the morning, the valley was unnaturally still.

Fargo made for Wilma's cabin. He didn't see a single soul anywhere yet he could feel eyes on him. He circled wide of the barn and the corral. The front door was open and someone was humming.

Reining up, Fargo swung his right leg over the saddle horn.

Never once taking his eyes off the door, he moved to one side of it and peered past the jamb.

Wilma was at the table, playing solitaire. She stopped humming and said without looking over, "You're welcome to come in, Mr. Fargo."

Quickly entering, Fargo put his back to the wall and covered her. "You were expecting me?"

"When I saw some of the menfolk come flyin' down off the mountain, I figured it hadn't gone well." Wilma hummed and set down another card.

"Do you want to hear about Garrick?"

"No. He's dead or you wouldn't be standin' there." Wilma sighed. "He was such a good son, too."

"He was a murdering bastard."

Wilma set down the deck and shifted in the chair to face him and laced her fingers in her lap. "Don't speak ill of the dead." She smiled sweetly. "Why did you come back, anyway? To shoot poor little me?"

Fargo sidled to the right so he could see both bedroom doors. They were shut. "Is anyone else here?"

"Aggy should be around somewhere. I haven't seen her in a while."

"She's up on the mountain."

Wilma stiffened in alarm. "She's not hurt, is she?"

Fargo took a few more steps. It put him midway between the two bedrooms and only a few feet from the table. "Your daughter is fine."

"Thank God." Wilma relaxed. "So what now, Mr. Scout?"

"Get on with it," Fargo said.

"I beg your pardon?"

"I don't have all day. You aim to kill me so go ahead and try."

Wilma's smile was plastered in place. "Wouldn't you rather have coffee? I know how much you like it."

"Stay where you are," Fargo warned.

Wilma got up.

24

Humming, Wilma stepped to the stove. She picked up the pot and shook it. "I'll have to put fresh on."

"What are you up to?" Fargo demanded. He was watching the bedroom doors. He thought he'd heard a slight sound but he couldn't be sure which bedroom it came from.

"I'm making you coffee." Wilma moved to the counter and filled the pot with water from the bucket. She opened the cupboard and took down the coffee and placed it next to the pot. "It won't take long. Have a seat if you'd like."

"Sit back down."

"You're not very sociable," Wilma said gaily.

Fargo marveled that she believed her playacting would fool him into lowering the Henry. Or maybe she didn't. Maybe she was only trying to distract him.

"I do so love tea more," Wilma prattled on. "Especially in the mornin' when I first wake up."

"Do you poison your own like you do others'?"

"Oh my," Wilma said. "So you figured that out, too? I had an idea you did."

The latch on the bedroom door on the right was slowly turning.

"Have you ever noticed that coffee drinkers are more irritable than tea drinkers? Why do you suppose that is? I have a theory. Tea calms the nerves but coffee agitates the system. Would you agree?"

Now the latch on the bedroom door on the left was slowly turning.

There were two of them, Fargo realized. He almost laughed. They thought they were being so clever. "Wilma?"

She stopped fiddling with the tea bags and looked up. In her left hand she held a wooden spoon. "Yes? Would you like some toast and jam too?"

"What signal did you agree on for them to try and kill me?"

Wilma couldn't hide her consternation. "I don't know what you're talkin' about."

"You told them you would offer to fix me some coffee," Fargo guessed. "Was that it?"

Wilma's eyes became flat and ugly. "I hate you more than I've ever hated anyone."

"Are they supposed to wait until I sit at the table? How will you let them know?"

"This way," Wilma said, and banged the wooden spoon against the coffeepot.

Both bedroom doors were flung open. Out of the room on the left sprang a Puma Fargo had never seen before, armed with a rifle. Out of the door on the right came Royal, the healer, a shotgun to his shoulder.

Fargo fired at the man on the left, and dived. As he hit the floor the shotgun boomed and the top of the table exploded.

He rolled and saw the man with the rifle was still on his feet and gamely trying to take aim. Fargo fired and the man staggered but still didn't go down. The muzzle of the man's rifle steadied, and Fargo sent a slug into his brainpan.

Royal came around the table in a rush, spewing cusswords in a spurt of breath.

Fargo rolled again.

The shotgun went off. Buckshot scoured the floorboards and Fargo felt a sting in his side. He fired into Royal's gut and the healer was jolted onto his heels. Royal had emptied both barrels and now he raised the shotgun like a club and charged, howling like a rabid wolf. Fargo fired without aiming and hit him in the neck, spinning him half around. Royal gagged, and spat blood, and clutched at a knife on his hip.

Fargo shot him in the face.

In the sudden silence Fargo heard his blood roaring in his veins. He examined his side and was relieved to discover he'd been only nicked. He placed the Henry's stock on the floor and was using the rifle to brace himself as he stood when shoes hammered and a screech tore the air.

Wilma's face was contorted in rage. She had a meat cleaver over her head and a butcher knife in her other hand.

Fargo brought the Henry up but he wasn't fast enough. He barely blocked the cleaver and lost his grip on the rifle. She slashed again, nearly taking off his fingers. He skipped back and clawed for his Colt and had to jerk his hand up as the butcher knife flashed.

Continuing to screech like a demented ghost, Wilma came after him. She swung the cleaver, the knife, the cleaver.

It was all Fargo could do not to be cut. He tried to dodge around her but the cleaver almost opened his neck. He went the other way and the butcher knife lanced at his groin. Bounding back, he collided with the wall.

A ghastly gleam came into Wilma's eyes. "I've got you now!" she exclaimed, and streaked the cleaver at his head.

Fargo ducked and heard the thunk of the blade as it bit into the wood. Lunging, he grabbed her other wrist, and wrenched. Wilma cried out. The knife slipped from her fingers and into Fargo's. He didn't hesitate. He drove the nine-inch blade up and in and swore he felt her heart strings sever.

Wilma gasped. Her mouth opened and blood gushed. She tottered, stared numbly at the knife hilt jutting from below her sternum, and folded in on herself like a human tent. She convulsed once, and was still.

"Damn," Fargo said. He moved to the Henry and bent to pick it up.

"Leave it there."

Fargo glanced at the front door.

Jonathan Coltraine was in the doorway, his twin Colts in his hands.

"What do you know," Fargo said.

"Straighten up," the gambler commanded, "and keep your hands where I can see them."

Fargo complied. He didn't try to stall as he had with Garrick and Wilma; Coltraine was too smart for that.

"You don't seem surprised."

"I'm not," Fargo said.

Coltraine entered and moved to one side. "What gave me away?"

"I didn't know for certain," Fargo admitted.

"There must have been something."

Fargo shrugged. "The Pumas weren't the forgiving kind, yet they let you live after you'd shot Chauncey. And they let you take up with one of their women when they hated outsiders. And then there was you and Wilma, huddled at the table when I came out of the bedroom."

"Chauncey got too big for his britches. He wanted a bigger cut. Wilma tried to talk him out of it but he came into town anyway."

"So you didn't shoot him over cheating at cards."

Coltraine smiled.

"And Garrick and his cousins taking shots at us? Was that your idea?"

"When I heard you were after the deserters, I didn't know if you were on to the Pumas. I arranged to make you think they were out for my blood so if you went after them, I could tag along." Coltraine wagged his Colts. "Unbuckle your gun belt and let it hit the floor."

Once more, Fargo did as he was told.

"Now sit in a chair facing the table with your hands behind the chair where I can reach them easy."

Fargo tempted fate by saying, "You're not going to gun me down where I stand?"

"I'm fixing to use you as bait."

Moving slowly so as not to draw a slug, Fargo eased into a chair. He watched as Coltraine moved over to Wilma, holstered a Colt, and yanked the butcher knife from her chest. One-handed, Coltraine jabbed the knife into her dress a few inches above the hem and made an opening big enough that he could slide his fingers through and tear off a long strip. The whole while, Coltraine kept one eye on him.

"Mind if we talk?"

"Not yet," Coltraine said. He strode up behind the chair, trailing the strip after him. "Face the table. You so much as move a muscle and I'll blow your brains out."

Fargo didn't doubt it. He sat there and submitted to having his wrists bound good and tight.

"That should do," Coltraine said. He came around the table, his Colts in their holsters, and went to the stove. "I could use some coffee."

"So could I. Wilma was about to put some on."

"I'm afraid you won't be having any this side of hell." Coltraine set about the task. "What did you want to talk about, as if I can't guess?"

"Are you a tit man or an ass man?"

Coltraine laughed. "I've got to hand it to you. You're as good as dead yet you can make jokes."

"What I'd like to know," Fargo said, "is how it all came about."

"By accident, more or less. I was on a long losing streak. That happens, you know. The cards go cold for days or sometimes weeks and it's all I can do to keep food in my belly." Coltraine paused. "As it happens, I was seeing Martha Puma at the time. You haven't met her yet, have you? She's as pretty a widow as you ever came across. I saw her in the general store one day and struck up a conversation. One thing led to another, and before long we were visiting each other in secret so her kin wouldn't find out she was fond of an outsider."

"What does your love life have to do with the deserters?"

"I'm getting to that. Be patient." Coltraine was filling the filter with coffee. "One night I was on my way out here and I crossed at the ferry with a gent in uniform. A corporal. He acted so nervous it made me wonder. And then when we got to the other side and he asked about the best trail through the Mountains of No Return, I knew he was a deserter."

"Finally," Fargo said.

"I told him that I didn't know about the trails but that Martha and her family would, and he rode along with me." Coltraine frowned. "If the damn fool hadn't confided in me that he was tired of the army and had saved a couple of hundred dollars to start over in civilian life, I wouldn't be standing here."

"You killed him for his money."

"I'm not proud of it," Coltraine said. "I waited until we were almost here and stuck my dagger in his ribs. I figured Martha would know a good place to bury the body, and she took me to the gully. Little did I suspect that once I'd gone, she'd go running to Wilma and spill all I'd done. Next thing I knew, Wilma and Garrick and a bunch of others showed up in town. They had a proposition for me."

"Hell," Fargo said.

Coltraine nodded. "They've always been poor, these Pumas. They think the rest of the world is against them and won't let them rise in life. But the truth is, they're too damn lazy to amount to much." He stared at Wilma's body. "She figured that with my help we could lure more deserters to their valley and dispose of them."

"You could have said no."

"I told you. The cards were against me. She agreed to split fifty-fifty and we both put up the money for the one man we needed to make sure our scheme worked."

"Who would that be?"

25

Jonathan Coltraine sat at the table facing the open front door. He had a pot of coffee beside him and was eating venison, potatoes, and carrots he'd cooked. "Martha will be here after a while. I'd like for you to meet her before you die."

Fargo was mildly surprised that the gambler was in such good spirits. Wilma, Garrick, Royal, Puce, and Lester and the rest of those in the gully were dead; all those who had been involved in the deserter-killing scheme. "You're taking this a lot better than I'd expect."

"You don't realize it," Coltraine said between mouthfuls, "but you've done me the biggest favor you could."

"How?" Fargo prompted when he didn't go on.

Coltraine speared a piece of carrot with his fork. "My luck has changed at the tables. I'm winning again. I've been thinking of taking Martha and leaving for Saint Louis or maybe New Orleans, but Wilma would have raised a stink. And since Martha wouldn't go against her wishes, I was stuck."

"And now you're not."

Coltraine beamed. "And now I'm not. And all thanks to you."

"You're welcome," Fargo said.

The gambler laughed. "You won't find it so funny when the other two show up."

"Which two?" Fargo asked, although he already knew.

"California Jim and that girl who's so fond of you. They're why you're still alive. As soon as I'm finished eating, I'm setting you out as bait, like I said I would."

Fargo was glad he'd told the pair to head for the fort if he didn't show up by morning. But he wasn't about to reveal that to Coltraine. "Why the girl?"

"She suspects what her mother and brother have been up to, and she knows I was involved with them. With her dead no one can connect me to any of it."

"You're one cold son of a bitch," Fargo said.

"I'll take that as a compliment." Coltraine chuckled. He looked toward the front door, and straightened. "Ah. Here she is now. Come in, my dear. Come in. Don't worry. He can't harm you."

The woman who entered was everything Coltraine had claimed.

Martha Puma was downright beautiful. She had long, full black hair, a body that any man would drool over, and the loveliest eyes. Her red lips were perpetually pouted as if she was about to bestow a kiss. The dress she wore clung to her as if it had been painted on. Warily eyeing him, she moved to the table and stood next to Coltraine and placed her arm on his shoulder.

"I waited as long as you told me."

"From here on out, we need never be separated again."

Martha was looking at the bodies. "He killed them, didn't he?"

"That he did. And now we're free."

Martha frowned at Wilma. "That old gal ran our family with an iron fist but she always did what was best for us. Her and Garrick, both."

"Forget about them." Coltraine set down his fork, pushed his chair back, and pulled Martha into his lap. Cupping her chin, he kissed her on the mouth and ran a hand down her hair.

"You shouldn't," she said. "Not with him watchin'." And she nodded at Fargo.

"Hell," Coltraine said. "How about we do it right here on the table?"

"I couldn't," Martha said. "As much as I like it, I can't in front of anybody."

"Too bad," Coltraine said. "It would amuse me no end." He raised her to her feet and smacked her fanny. "Gather up the guns on the floor, if you would. I'm almost done and we have to get ready for our guests."

"Guests?" Martha said.

"The last two who have to die before we can begin our new life free and clear."

"Who has to die?" Martha asked as she moved to the shotgun Royal Puma had dropped.

"The one they call California Jim, and Aggy."

Martha stopped. "Agatha? Why do we have to kill her?"

Coltraine forked venison into his mouth and chewed. "She knows too much."

"But she's sweet as can be. She always treats me nice. I like her."

"Would you rather see me dangling from a rope?"

"Maybe she doesn't know as much as you think she does," Martha said. "Maybe we can spare her."

"You might be willing to take the chance," Coltraine said. "I'm not."

Fargo had an inspiration. Clearing his throat, he said to Martha, "It makes you wonder, doesn't it? Who he might be willing to kill to keep from being hung?"

Coltraine stopped chewing. "That was dirty." He turned to his lover. "Don't listen to him. He's trying to turn you against me. You know how much I care. I'd never in a million years harm a hair on your head."

Martha gnawed her lower lip.

"Did you hear me?"

"I heard you," Martha replied. She broke the shotgun open and ejected the spent shells. Bending, she patted Royal's pockets, found more, and reloaded both barrels.

"Nice try," Coltraine said to Fargo, "but Martha and I have been together too long for her to fall for your tricks. Fact is, once we reach wherever we end up, I aim to make her my wife. Don't I, sweetheart?"

"So you've promised me," Martha said.

"I'm a man of my word," Coltraine said. "We'll set up house and I'll make a good living at the tables and you can wear pretty dresses and go to the theater and live the life you've always hankered after."

"I would love to live in a city," Martha said. "All the things I've read about it, it sounds elegant."

"You hear that?" Coltraine said to Fargo. "Elegant?" And he laughed.

"So long as you're happy together," Fargo said, and looked at Martha. "But you know how men are. What if he tires of you some day? What if he decides that you know too much, like Aggy? What then?"

Coltraine slammed his fist down so hard, the whole table shook. "Enough, damn you! I won't have you souring her against me. One more goddamn word and I'll gag you, you son of a bitch."

Fargo didn't press his luck. He'd planted a seed and now Martha had a slightly troubled expression. "What happens if California and Aggy never show up?"

"They will," Coltraine said confidently. "California wouldn't run out on you. And the girl can't keep her eyes off you, handsome devil that you are."

Fargo inwardly smiled at the disappointment the gambler was in for. "Seeing your neck stretched on a gallows would make my day."

"That's never going to happen," Coltraine said. "I'll do whatever it takes to make sure it doesn't."

Fargo almost laughed when Martha shot him a sharp look. "This man you say that you paid to help make your scheme work, is he in the army or in town?"

"Neither," Coltraine said, and caught himself. "Damn you. Bring it up again and I'll take a rifle stock to your teeth."

Fargo fell silent. He had to figure a way out of this mess. The Arkansas toothpick was still in his ankle sheath. If Coltraine and Martha left him alone long enough he could cut himself free. "You know," he said to the gambler, "there's a nice, soft bed in Wilma's room for you two to fool around on."

Coltraine pushed his plate back and took a handkerchief from a pocket and wiped his mouth. "And have your friends show up while we were going at it? I don't think so."

Martha had placed the shotgun on the table and gone to the rifle near the other man. She picked it up and set it next to the shotgun. "Maybe I should go back to my place."

"Why?" Coltraine asked.

"I don't like killin'. And I don't care to be a party to Aggy's. I told you. I like her."

"You can go in one of the bedrooms," Coltraine said. "You don't have to see."

"I'd hear it," Martha said. "That would be just as awful."

"I thought we'd talked all this out. I thought you agreed on what I had to do."

"I didn't know about Aggy," Martha said.

"Do you love me or don't you?" Coltraine demanded.

"I do."

"Then quit your damn bellyaching and trust me. I'd never do anything to cause you hurt."

"I'd like to think that," Martha said.

Coltraine turned toward Fargo and sighed. "Women. You can't live without them and you can't throw them off cliffs."

"*You* could," Fargo said. "Anyone who could kill a sweet girl like Aggy wouldn't have any qualms about killing someone else."

A flush of anger spread up Coltraine's face. Standing, he came around the table and over to the chair and lashed out with his fist.

Fargo's jaw rocked with pain. He tasted blood in his mouth but didn't black out.

"I warned you," Coltraine said. He picked up the shotgun and the rifle and took them into Wilma's bedroom. When he came back, he went to Martha and embraced her. "In you go. Shut the door. I'll stay out here and take care of everything. By nightfall we'll be on our way."

"What if someone comes by and sees Wilma and them lyin' there? Someone who doesn't know about the deserters?"

"I'll take care of that, too." Coltraine kissed her and ushered her to Wilma's bedroom and shut the door.

Fargo hadn't thought much about the other Pumas but now he did. He wondered how many were like Aggy, ignorant of the goings-on.

Coltraine began dragging the bodies into the other bedroom. First it was Wilma. She was so heavy, he puffed some and stopped once to catch his breath. Coming back out, he dragged the healer off and finally the last man. Closing the bedroom door, he brushed at his frock coat and came over to the chair.

"Now it's your turn."

"The times I've played cards with you," Fargo said, "I'd never have taken you for the bastard you are."

Coltraine frowned. "If I hadn't had that long run of bad luck, I wouldn't have murdered anyone. To tell the truth, I always thought of myself as honest and upright."

"You're a piece of shit."

The gambler glowered and cocked his fist but didn't swing. "No, you don't. I'm not letting you get my goat again."

"The truth hurts, they say."

Suddenly gripping the back of the chair, Coltraine tilted it and dragged it to the center of the room and turned it so Fargo faced the front door. "There. The first thing they see when they look in will be you." He pulled out the handkerchief he'd used to wipe his mouth. "Open wide."

"Like hell."

Coltraine drew his right Colt. "I can pistol-whip you and do it anyway."

Fargo opened wide and moved his tongue to the side of his mouth.

"Smart man." Coltraine wadded the handkerchief and carefully shoved it in. "There. Spit it out and I'll be mad, and you don't want me mad." He patted Fargo on the shoulder. "Now all we do is wait. Enjoy the time you have left. As soon as they show up, you're dead."

26

Half the afternoon was gone. Fargo's wrists hurt from the tight cloth and his mouth was dry from the gag. His jaw bothered him, too. His only consolation was that Coltraine wouldn't get to kill California and Aggy because they weren't coming.

The gambler was at the table playing poker against himself with Wilma's cards. Now and then he glanced at the front door, and frowned. He was growing impatient.

Fargo sat quietly. There hadn't been a peep out of Martha, and he wondered if she had lain down and fallen asleep.

More time passed, and Coltraine slapped down the cards and stood. "What the hell is taking them so long? I figured they'd be here by now." He stalked to the chair, reached two fingers in, and yanked out the gag. "Where are they?"

"How would I know?" Fargo said. "The last I saw, they were up the gully past the graves."

Coltraine went to the front door and gazed up and down the valley. "Something isn't right. I get the feeling you're lying to me."

"You should get Martha and light a shuck while you still can."

His mouth a slit, Coltraine came back. "I have half a mind to gun you where you sit."

"That would be your style," Fargo said.

Coltraine was mad. He stomped to Wilma's bedroom and reached for the latch, saying, "Martha? You can come out if you want." He opened the door, and froze, his mouth agape. "What the hell?" he blurted. Whirling, he ran past Fargo and out the front door.

Instantly, Fargo bent his legs back as far as they would go and groped at his right pant leg. He got it up over the boot and was about to slide his fingers in and palm the toothpick when footsteps warned him to sit up.

Coltraine came back in, looking bewildered. "She's gone," he said. "She slipped out the window and must have gone to her place."

"She told you she didn't want any part of this."

"Don't remind me," Coltraine snapped. "Damn her. I had this all worked out and she goes and pulls a stunt like this."

"Your lover might be having second thoughts about you." Fargo rubbed it in.

"Shut the hell up." Coltraine placed his hands on his Colts and set to pacing. "I should go talk to her but I can't leave until California and Aggy show up."

"Sure you can," Fargo said. "I won't mind."

The gambler stopped and turned toward the front door. "Wait. Do you hear that?"

Belatedly, Fargo did; the distant drum of hooves. Surely not, he told himself, and broke out in a cold sweat.

Coltraine smiled and drew his Colts. "At last." He darted over behind the front door and cocked both revolvers. "It took them long enough."

The drumming grew louder. From the sound, there were two horses.

Fargo pictured California on his and Aggy on her brother's.

Surely not, he told himself again.

Coltraine had his ear to the crack between the door and jamb. "It won't be long now," he gloated.

The horses rumbled to a halt outside and the last voice Fargo wanted to hear gave a holler.

"Pard? Are you in there?"

Fargo wanted to hit him.

"It's me, California. Come on out if it's safe."

Coltraine was peering out the crack, trying to see them.

Fargo raised his head. The gambler had forgotten that he'd taken the gag out. "It's not safe!" he shouted. "Coltraine is behind all the killings, and he's waiting for you!"

Coltraine spun. Fury lit his eyes and he leveled both Colts.

Fargo braced for the impact of the slugs but for some reason the gambler didn't shoot.

Outside, a commotion erupted. Saddles creaked and feet padded.

Coltraine seemed to be struggling to control his temper. "California, you hear me?" he yelled.

"I hear you, you buzzard."

"I want you to lay down your guns and come in empty-handed or I shoot Fargo."

"You got that backward," California hollered. "I've got the front covered and Aggy has the back. *You* come out with your hands empty and maybe I'll let you live."

"Don't you care that Fargo will die?"

"Sure I care. But I ain't dumb enough to throw away the only chance we have of savin' his hide."

"Goddamn it," Coltraine said to himself. "Nothing is going as it should."

"More of that bad luck of yours," Fargo said.

"Shut up." Coltraine shoved the front door half shut and ran to Wilma's bedroom. He was in there less than a minute, and when he came back out he was grumbling, ". . . out there behind the outhouse with her damn Sharps."

"Sounds like they have you boxed in," Fargo said.

"I told you to shut up." Coltraine went to the front door but didn't show himself. "California?"

"What do you want, you backstabbing son of a bitch?"

"I'll make a deal with you."

"As if I'd trust you, you bastard."

"If you can stop insulting me long enough to listen, there's a way all of us can get out of this alive. Including Fargo."

"I'm listening, you skunk."

"Aggy and you pull back out of rifle range. I'll bring Fargo out the front where you can see him. Then I'll climb on my horse and go and leave him for you to untie." When no answer was forthcoming, Coltraine snapped, "Well? What's it to be?"

"I don't know," California said. "What does he say?"

The gambler looked at Fargo. "It's either that or I gun you and take my chances with them. Make up your mind. I want to get the hell out of here."

Fargo suspected it was a trick. Coltraine was giving up too easily. He hesitated.

Coltraine misconstrued his silence. "To hell with you, then. I'll do it my way." He came around the chair and tilted it back.

"What are you up to?"

"Saving my hide." Turning, Coltraine dragged the chair to the front door, and paused. "I'm bringing him out. Hold your fire."

"The army and the federal marshals will be after you," Fargo said. "Where can you go?"

"Out of the country if I have to," Coltraine said. He backed out of the door, pulling the chair after him. When he had gone a few feet he turned the chair around, let go, and ran back inside.

Twenty yards out, California Jim rose from a patch of high grass, his rifle to his shoulder. "Pard?" he called uncertainly.

"Stay there." Fargo looked over his shoulder. He suspected that Coltraine might be waiting to shoot California when he came close but he didn't see the gambler anywhere.

"Pard?" California said again.

"I don't think it's—" Fargo said, and got no further.

From the rear of the cabin came the crash of pistols, two shots followed by a piercing wail.

"No!" Fargo cried, and struggled frantically at the cloth that bound his wrists. He could resort to his toothpick but it would take too long. There was a faster way. "California! Come quick and cut me free!"

His friend was already barreling toward him.

On the side of the cabin a horse whinnied. Hooves hammered, fading rapidly to the east.

California had his big knife out and didn't waste a second. He ran behind the chair and slashed twice. "There you go, pard."

Fargo leaped up.

"I hope that scream wasn't what I think it was."

So did Fargo. He raced around the cabin. His wrists hurt like hell but he ignored them.

The sight that met his eyes chilled his blood.

"God, no."

Aggy lay on her back midway between the outhouse and the cabin. Her arms were outflung and her fingers were twitching and curling.

Fargo ran to her. Two dark stains on her buckskin shirt told him all there was to know. Her eyes were open and fixed on the sky and pink froth was curdling from the corners of her mouth. Sinking to his knees, he gently cradled her head. "Aggy?" he said softly.

California caught up and lurched to a stop. "Damn him to hell," he said. "Not her."

"Aggy?" Fargo said again.

She blinked a few times, and coughed, and her eyes swiveled in their sockets but couldn't seem to find him. "Skye?"

"I'm here," Fargo said.

"I heard shoutin' and was comin' to see what was goin' on, and there that fancy gambler was, half out the bedroom window. He up and shot me."

Fargo remembered their lovemaking, and how she tried to stop her brother in the gully, and the ice in his veins became molten lava.

"He didn't give me no warnin' or nothin'." Aggy coughed. "He just shot me."

"He'll get his," Fargo vowed. He caressed her hair and she reached up and clutched his hand. "I'm all woozy, Skye. I can't hardly think."

"Lie quiet," Fargo said.

"I'm done for, ain't I?"

Helplessness washed over Fargo, and he bit off a string of oaths.

"You can be honest with me," Aggy said. "Is there anythin' you can do?"

"No."

"I'm sorry, girlie," California said. "I shouldn't have let you watch the back of the cabin."

"Who else was there?" Aggy said. "And it was my idea, remember?" She coughed some more and the pink froth became a bright red.

"And to think we trusted him," California said.

"He used us," Fargo said. "From the very beginning."

"I never did like that hombre," Aggy said weakly. "Until he came along our family was doin' fine."

Fargo rubbed her arm and her shoulder. "Would you like a drink of water?"

"What I'd like," Aggy said, "is for you to hold me good and tight."

As carefully as he could, Fargo raised her higher and hugged her.

Aggy pressed her cheek to his chest and closed her eyes. "This is nice."

"I can't stand to watch," California said, and he walked a dozen feet off.

"He's such a dear," Aggy said. She gave a mild start. "Say, how's Ma, anyhow? I didn't think to ask."

"She fine," Fargo lied.

"Why ain't she here?"

"Coltraine tied her up."

"Send California to free her. I'd like to see her one more time before I—" Aggy straightened, gasped, and died.

Fargo held her a long while.

27

Fargo stopped at three cabins before he was told where Martha Puma lived. The first two cabins, he galloped up with California Jim, vaulted down, and pounded on the front doors. No one came. He tried to open the doors but they were bolted.

At the second cabin a man nervously shouted at him to go away, warning he had a rifle.

At the third, Fargo wasn't off the Ovaro when an elderly lady with white hair, wearing an apron, opened the front door and smiled at him. "How do, stranger."

"You're awful friendly for a Puma," Fargo growled.

"And you sound awful mad."

"Aggy Puma has been killed," Fargo said. "I'm after the bastard who did it. Where does Martha live?"

"Martha?" The woman frowned. "Then it must be that man of hers, that outsider."

"Which cabin?"

The old woman pointed. "Two more and you'll be there. She has a little yellow windmill out in front. She's fond of windmills."

Fargo went to rein away.

"I never did cotton to him. They say he loves her but anyone could tell he was only after one thing."

A jab of Fargo's spurs and he was at a gallop again. California rode grimly at his side. They swept past the two cabins the woman had mentioned and ahead was one with a small yellow windmill. Smoke curled from the chimney. The corral at the rear held a single horse.

"He's not there," California shouted.

Fargo stopped anyway. He shook the door with his blows until finally the bolt was thrown and Martha Puma opened it.

She had been crying. Her eyes were moist, her cheeks streaked, and she was wringing a white cloth in her hands.

"You," she said simply.

"Where is he?"

"He didn't kill you," Martha said.

Fargo grabbed her arm. "Where the hell is he?"

"He was here but he left," Martha said, and more tears trickled. "It's over between us."

"Which way did he go?"

"He came all in a rush," Martha said, staring blankly off into space. "Told me he had to light a shuck and would I go with him? I said I couldn't just up and leave. I have my cabin and my cats and the canary he brought me when I said I like birds."

"Where, damn it?"

"Do you know what he did?" Martha looked at him. "He told me I had to make up my mind. I could go with him now or I could stay here and rot. His very words. Stay here and rot." She broke down sobbing and pressed the cloth to her face.

Fargo was at the end of his patience. He was about to shake her to get it out of her when California Jim came up, took his hand off her arm, and enfolded her shoulders in one of his.

"There, there, ma'am. I don't blame you for being upset. He shouldn't ought to have done that."

Martha nodded and sniffled. "After all our time together. After I gave myself to him, heart and soul. How can he discard me like I'm used dishwater?"

"He's a polecat, that one," California said. "My pard and me would like to get our hands on him if you can point us in the direction he took."

"East," Martha said. "When I looked out he was headin' for Hadleyville."

"Thank you, ma'am," California said. "You've been a big help."

Fargo and California turned to go.

"He made a strange comment," Martha said, talking to the air more than to them.

Fargo stopped. "Strange how?"

"He went to the door and stood there and I heard him say he had a card to play that could trump the deck. Then he went out and I heard him ride off."

"What in tarnation could that have meant?" California Jim wondered.

They pushed to overtake Coltraine but after an hour it was obvious they wouldn't before sunset. Reluctantly, as the last light faded, Fargo stopped. Riding in the mountains at night was dangerous enough. With Utes on the prowl, that danger was compounded.

California Jim saw to the fire and the coffee and even made a stew of flour and pemmican. They ate in silence until California said, "What do you aim to do to him once we catch him?"

"You need to ask?"

"He done for Aggy and deserves it, I reckon," California said. "I just figured you might want him alive to hand over to Colonel Williams."

"What for? We know where the deserters got to."

"True," California said. "But maybe the colonel would want to question him anyway."

"Tough," Fargo said.

"It's Aggy, ain't it? What he did to her?"

"He played us for jackasses."

"But it's Aggy, mostly. She was sweet on you and I know how you are."

Fargo stared across the fire. "How am I?"

"You're as hard as flint," California said, "except when you're not."

"That's no answer."

"You want particulars? Fine." California extended a finger as he rattled off, "You can't stand to see a wrong done to anyone. You like women and poker and whiskey but you have more honor in you than most churchgoers. You have grit, and you have a temper. Mostly, though, you're your own man, and you won't be pushed, bullied, or put-upon. Oh. And you can't keep your cock in your pants."

Fargo nearly snorted stew out his nose when he burst into laughter. "Damn you."

"So do I know you or not?"

"Not," Fargo said with a grin.

"I know you won't rest until Jon Coltraine has gone under," California said. "Even if it takes the rest of your days to find him."

"It won't take that long."

"The head start he has, we might not catch him."

"Remember what Martha said," Fargo reminded him.

California scrunched up his face in puzzlement. "About him having a card that could trump us?"

Fargo nodded.

"His card could be anything. Maybe he has some friends who will help him gun us. Or it could just be he'll change his name and head east and disappear."

"It's not any of that," Fargo said.

"You think you know what it is?"

"I have a suspicion," Fargo said.

"Care to share?"

"Coltraine dropped a few words about someone he needed to make his scheme work and there's only one person I can think of who fits. But I could be wrong."

California didn't press it. They finished their meal and sat sipping coffee and listening to the coyotes and the wolves and once the roar of a bear.

"All those soldier-boys," California said out of the blue.

"They brought it on themselves."

"By deserting? Hell, you heard the colonel. Hundreds do it every year and don't end up like them. And it's not as if they died in battle. Being poisoned is a hell of a way to go. I should know. I almost was."

The fiery streak of a shooting star brought their conversation to an end. Shortly after, California Jim turned in.

Fargo stayed up. Whether it was from the day's events or all the coffee, he wasn't tired. He hoped he was wrong about his suspicion because if he was right there may be more blood spilled than just Coltraine's.

By midnight Fargo was yawning. By one he had lain on his side and was waiting for sleep to claim him. Right before it did, he thought he glimpsed a fire, far off. Coltraine, he figured.

Well before daybreak Fargo was up and had rekindled the coffee. He looked for the far-off fire but no luck. When a touch of yellow infused the horizon, he kicked California's boots.

Snorting and muttering, California raised his head and looked about. "I do not approve," he said, and lay back down.

"Get your carcass up," Fargo said. "We have a lot of riding to do."

Inside the hour they were on their way. Fargo led down a long slope littered with boulders to a bench above a wide valley. He was about to descend when movement caused him to imitate a tree.

Riders had come out of the timber on the valley floor. Ten, all told, their feathers and their bows and arrows leaving no doubt who they were and what they were.

"Into the trees," Fargo directed.

They made it undetected. Dismounting, Fargo moved to where he could see the valley, and hunkered. To his annoyance the Utes had stopped.

"What are they up to?" California said. "We can't go on until they leave."

One of the warriors climbed down and checked a hoof on his mount. Apparently it was fine because he swung back on and the war party departed to the north.

Fargo waited a while before he descended. Invisible needles prickling his skin, he crossed the open space to the next stretch of dense timber.

"Whew," California Jim exhaled as the trees closed around them.

Several miles farther they were climbing yet another ridge when the Ovaro nickered and pricked its ears and California's mount shied.

"What the hell?"

Fargo was intent on a patch of aspens the Ovaro was staring at. Something was in there. Something big. A dark bulk appeared, its nose to the ground. It was almost out of the aspens when it raised its head and spotted them and let out a loud woof.

"It's only a black bear," California Jim said in relief.

Fargo stayed where he was. Black bears usually ran at the sight of humans. But not always. And this one was as big as a small griz. He placed his hand on the stock of his Henry, ready to whip it from the scabbard if need be.

The black bear reared onto its hind legs.

"Oh hell," California said. "It better not be thinking to do what I think it is. Want me to shoot into the ground to scare it off?"

"The Utes might hear. Just sit still."

Raising its head, the black bear sniffed and *woofed* again and dropped onto all fours.

"It better not," California said.

It didn't. Wheeling, the bear loped off through the aspens and was soon out of sight.

That was the last incident until they came to the overlook above the Agate River, and the ferry.

"We're almost to Hadleyville and there's been no sign of Coltraine yet," California Jim said, his disappointment plain. "I hate to think he'll get away."

"He won't," Fargo said.

"We'll ask the ferryman how long ago Coltraine crossed," California said.

"We'll do more than that," Fargo said, and made sure his Colt was loose in its holster.

28

Fargo drew rein at the landing on the west side of the river. The ferry was on the east side, unattended. A rope had been rigged, attached to a bell. To get the ferryman's attention, all someone had to do was tug on the rope. Dismounting, he went to the pole and pulled. He was at it for a couple of minutes before the door to the tavern opened and out came Milner.

"It took him long enough," California Jim grumbled.

Another man emerged from the tavern. Younger than Milner, he had a similar build and wore similar clothes.

"That must be the son that that gal Edith told us about," California said.

Father and son went to the ferry and presently were under way.

It seemed to Fargo that it was taking them twice as long to cross as it did the last time.

California Jim noticed, too. "Hell, if they went any slower, they wouldn't get here until next year."

"Don't turn your back to them," Fargo said.

"How's that?"

"Keep your hand close to your six-shooter and don't let either of them get behind you."

"Why not?"

"Remember I told you that I suspect someone?"

"You suspect Milner?"

"Think about it. The ferryman is the one person who could let Coltraine know when deserters were on their way up into the mountains."

"But how would the ferryman know they *were* deserters? It's not as if they'd come right out and say so."

"Soldiers never go into the Mountains of No Return except on patrol. If one showed up here alone, or maybe with a couple of friends, it'd stand to reason what they were up to."

Milner and the son continued to pull toward shore.

"It could be," Fargo speculated, "the ferryman is the one who steers them toward Wilma and her kin. Coltraine told me that she and him paid someone to help them."

"I'll be damned," California said. "And if Coltraine has already been here and warned Milner . . ." He didn't finish.

Fargo nodded.

"We could be wrong," California said. "It could be someone else is working for that son of a bitch."

"We'll find out soon enough," Fargo said. "If the Milners are in it with him, they won't let us live to reach the other side."

California placed his right hand on his holster. "Wonderful. And I can't swim worth a lick."

Presently the ferry was near enough that Milner called out to them. "Back so soon, are you?" He elaborated when the ferry bumped against the landing and his son had tied it off. "I seem to recollect you mentioning that you were heading clear through to the other side of the mountains."

"We have to get to Fort Barker," Fargo told him to see how he would react.

"You make it sound urgent," Milner said.

"It is."

"Well, come aboard, and me and Seth, here, will have you across in no time."

Seth stayed by the rail. Despite the summer weather he was wearing a coat that bulged on his left hip. "How do," he said.

Fargo led the Ovaro on. The stallion had taken so many ferry trips that it never gave him a problem. But California Jim's animal balked. California had to pat it and softly cajole it before it would cooperate.

They got under way, father and son at the rope.

Milner was in a gabby mood. "I've sure been having a lot of people cross of late."

"All the better for your poke," California said.

Milner chuckled. "I do like money. Which reminds me. That gent you were with crossed over last night. Your gambler friend."

"About what time?" Fargo asked.

"Late," Milner said. "After dark, it was. I hollered across that I don't usually ferry folks after the sun goes down and he'd have to wait until morning. But he offered me twice the rate so I brought him over."

"Generous of him," Fargo said.

"You ask me, he was in a powerful hurry," Milner said. "He acted nervous, too."

California said, "I wonder why."

"I don't pry."

Fargo turned his left side to the Milners so he could rest his hand on his Colt without the pair noticing.

The ferry reached the halfway point. Fargo figured that if anything was going to happen it would be soon.

"Run into any redskins while you were up in the high country?" Milner asked.

"I thought you don't pry," California said.

"Not into personal stuff, no," Milner said. "But the folks who cross like to hear if the Utes are acting up."

"They are," Fargo confirmed.

"Damn. The government should round them all up and put them on a reservation and keep them there. Or wipe them out."

"The women and children too?" California said.

"Why not?" Milner rejoined. "The women bring more into the world. And the gnats grow up to take white hair."

Fargo almost wished the ferryman would try something. He hated bigots as much as he hated anything.

"Yes, sir," Milner said, "the West will be a better place when the last hostile has been sent to hell."

"That's enough about Indians," California Jim declared.

"You're not one of them Injun lovers, are you?"

"Enough means enough," California said.

The rest of the crossing was conducted in silence. The ferry bumped and Milner and Seth secured it and arranged the plank.

"Off you go," Milner said. "And if you're thirsty, you're welcome to stop at my tavern."

"You first," Fargo said.

Milner gave his son a sharp glance, and nodded. Together they went down the plank.

Fargo led the Ovaro off. He flicked his eyes from the Milners to the tavern. A curtain in the tavern window moved.

He waited for California and when his friend was at his side, he said, "Maybe we'll have a drink, after all."

Milner smiled. "My gal Edith is at the bar. Go right on in and she'll fix you up."

"You first," Fargo said again.

Milner gave a mild start. "Thanks for the invite. But I don't want a drink right now."

"Sure you do."

Milner looked worried. "You can't force a man to drink if he doesn't want to, mister."

"Head for the tavern anyway. You and your son, both."

Seth moved his coat, revealing a Starr revolver worn for a cross-draw.

"What's gotten into you?" Milner asked. "What's this about, anyhow?"

Without taking his eyes off them, Fargo handed the Ovaro's reins to California. "Stay out here and watch our horses."

"I'll be damned if I will," California said.

"I wasn't asking."

"I'm your pard, damn you," California said. "Boss them if you want but you don't boss me."

"It's best if you do," Fargo insisted.

"Give me one good reason."

"I need you to watch my back."

"How can I do that out here?"

"Do it over by the door," Fargo said, "in case there are others." He thought it unlikely but California had already been wounded and near-poisoned.

"I suppose that's reason enough," California said, "but I sure as hell don't like it."

Fargo focused on the Milners. "Now then. Where were we?" He smiled. "We were about to go in your tavern. Whether you want to or not."

Seth's jaw muscles hardened and he looked at his father, who was a study in bewilderment. "Pa?" he said.

"We do as he says."

"But, Pa—" Seth protested.

Milner cut him short with a gesture. "You do as I tell you, you hear? My gut tells me we go against him and we're dead."

"How good can he be?" Seth said.

Before the father could reply, Fargo said, "Go for your six-gun."

"Huh?" Seth said.

"Try to draw it."

Seth hesitated, then quickly moved his hand toward the Starr. Fargo's Colt was out and cocked before Seth touched it.

Seth froze, his mouth agape, his face draining of color.

"Sweet Jesus."

"I told you, son," Milner said.

"Use two fingers," Fargo directed, "and set it on the ground."

Seth hastily obeyed, and raised his arms.

"Head for the tavern," Fargo said, and twirled the Colt into his holster. "When we get there, go to the first table and sit."

Father and son walked side by side. Milner opened the door and held it and Seth entered.

Fargo slipped in after them and immediately stepped to the right.

Edith was at the bar, cleaning glasses. She looked over at her father and brother and her brow knit.

"Pa? What's going on?"

"Hush and stay where you are," Milner commanded.

Behind the bar was a hallway into the house. The hallway was dark.

Beginning to think he was wrong, feeling like a fool, Fargo said to the darkness, "You can come out."

For long seconds nothing happened. Then the dark shifted and out strolled Jonathan Coltraine with his thumbs hooked in his gun belt. "How did you know?"

"It's where I would be," Fargo said.

Coltraine smiled at Edith and came around the end of the bar and stood with his back to the corner. "I should have known I couldn't count on you," he said to the father and the son.

"He never gave us the chance," Milner said. "And besides, gun work wasn't part of our agreement."

Coltraine sighed. "If you want something done," he said, squaring his shoulders. "Where's California?"

"Outside," Fargo said.

"Good. When I'm done with you I'll take care of him." Coltraine parted his frock coat wider and lowered his arms to his sides.

"Pa," Edith said in amazement. "They're fixing to shoot it out."

"Hush, I said, girl."

Fargo concentrated on Coltraine and only Coltraine. When the gambler's hands flashed, he flashed his hand. When the gambler's Colts leaped up and out, so did his Colt. It was his that thundered first. Fargo heard the buzz of lead past his ear and he fired again, and yet a third time. Coltraine rocked on his heels, fell into the corner, and made one more effort to shoot.

Fargo shot him between the eyes.

The door burst in and California was there with his revolver out. He stopped and blurted, "I'll be damned. Is it over, then?"

Fargo nodded at the Milners. "We take them to Colonel Williams and it will be."

"What then, pard?"

"I think," Skye Fargo said, "I'll stay drunk for a week."

LOOKING FORWARD!
The following is the opening
section of the next novel in the exciting
Trailsman series from Signet:

TRAILSMAN #367
TEXAS TEMPEST

*The wilds of West Texas, 1861—where certain
death waited for the unwary.*

The fight just sort of happened.

Skye Fargo was at the bar of the Zachary Saloon when one of
three rowdy men next to him bumped his arm. He was jostled so
hard, whiskey spilled over his chin and down his shirt. He glared
at the man but the three ignored him. They were drunk, and laughing and joking and pushing one another.

Fargo's temper flared. A big man, broad of shoulder and narrow
at the waist, he wore buckskins and a red bandanna, and a Colt
high on his hip. He set down his glass, and swore.

The three had polished off a bottle and were working on the
second. By their clothes they were laborers, several of the many
workers on the new buildings going up. Corpus Christi, Texas, was
growing by the proverbial leaps and bounds.

"Watch what you're doing, you jackass," Fargo growled, and
motioned at the bartender for a refill.

The man who had jostled him turned. He was a block of muscle with a square chin covered with stubble. "Were you talkin' to me?"

Fargo gestured at the wet stain on his shirt and wiped his dripping chin with his sleeve. "I sure as hell am."

"What did I do?"

"Are you blind? You made me spill my drink." Fargo figured that was the end of it and faced the bar. He was wrong. The man poked his shoulder.

"Don't talk to me like that and then turn away. I don't like it."

"I don't give a good damn what you like," Fargo told him.

The man placed his big hands on his hips and puffed out his chest. "You hear this bastard, boys? Sayin' I pushed him."

The other two moved closer to their friend. One had beetling brows and the other a crooked nose.

"Even if you did, Jacob, he had no call to insult you," beetling brows said.

Crooked nose nodded. "You ask me, he should apologize."

"You hear that?" Jacob said to Fargo. "Say you're sorry."

"Like hell," Fargo said. "You bumped me. I didn't bump you."

"You called me a jackass."

"I take it back."

"You do?"

Fargo nodded. He knew he shouldn't say what he was about to but he couldn't help himself. "You're a dumb son of a bitch who doesn't know when to leave well enough be."

A flush spread up Jacob's face. "Is that so?" he grated.

"I think you should buy me a drink to make up for the one you made me spill."

"Is that so?" Jacob said again, and glanced at his companions. "Do you want to know what I think?" He didn't wait for them to answer. "I think we should pound this gent into the floor."

"Maybe break a few bones while we're at it," beetling brows said.

"And then throw him out back with the trash," crooked nose chimed in.

Jacob smiled and smacked his right fist into his left palm. "Who wants to start the fun?"

"I do," Fargo said, and unleashed an uppercut that tilted Jacob onto his heels. A left cross sent him crashing onto a table.

For a few seconds the other two were rooted in stunned disbelief, which was all the opening Fargo needed to wade in and let fly with a flurry of jabs that drove both men stumbling back. He slammed a solid right to beetling brow's jaw, spun, and drove his left fist deep into crooked nose's gut.

All three were down but they didn't stay there. Bellowing like a mad bull, Jacob heaved to his feet and lumbered at Fargo with his fists cocked. The bartender yelled something about not damaging the place. Fargo ducked an awkward looping right, delivered a powerful left, evaded another swing, and connected with a knuckle-buster to the chin.

Jacob crashed down a second time.

The others were rising. Boiling fury blazed in their eyes.

Fargo didn't let them set themselves. He was on them in a whirlwind of blows, his arms like steam-engine pistons. He broke the crooked nose and pulped a beetling brow.

Fargo's right hand hurt like hell but he ignored the pain. He stood over the three, poised to tear into them again should it be necessary. "No more," he warned. "Let it drop."

The other patrons had stopped what they were doing to gape. Fistfights weren't all that common. Most Texans settled disputes with their six-shooters.

Out in the street a wagon clattered.

Jacob slowly sat up. He rubbed his jaw and looked at his friends and they looked at him and all three nodded.

"Hell," Fargo said.

In unison they came up and simultaneously attacked.

Fargo blocked, countered, gave way. He'd been in more than his share of barroom brawls but three at once were too many and some of their punches slipped through. His left cheek exploded in pain. His temple was clipped. A boot arced at his groin and he narrowly avoided it. He kept on retreating and then suddenly he was against a wall and they had him half-ringed.

"Now we've got him," Jacob snarled.

Not if Fargo could help it. Rather than be overwhelmed, he

went at them, hitting hard, hitting fast, first one man and then another. In their drunken state they were sluggish. It cost them. He bloodied a mouth, rammed his fist into an eye, split an ear. A knee arced at his manhood. Sidestepping, he planted the toe of his boot between Jacob's legs. The man with the busted nose lunged, seeking to wrap his bony fingers around his neck; Fargo gave him a straight-arm to the face that felled him where he stood.

Only one of the drunks was still on his feet and he was the fastest. He slipped a cross that should have laid him out and retaliated with short blows thrown at Fargo's eyes. Tucking at the knees, Fargo rammed his fist up under the man's sternum. Beetling brow folded in on himself and lay in a heap.

Fargo was breathing heavily. His temple was sore and his ribs were hurting. He waited for them to resume the fight but all three stayed on the floor. Realizing it was over, he went to the bar and gulped the refill.

"That was some fist-slingin'," the bartender said by way of praise.

Fargo tapped the glass. "Another."

"Serves them right," the bartender said as he took a bottle from a shelf. "But you might want to skedaddle in case the sheriff shows up."

Fargo didn't see how the sheriff could blame him for any of it but he had somewhere to be, anyway, so he nodded, drained the glass, and paid.

"Come again," the bartender said.

Corpus Christi had grown since Fargo was there last. About twenty years ago there was nothing but a trading post. Then a few settlers moved in, and the army came and stayed a while, and before long a small town sprang up. Thanks to the bay, ships were constantly coming and going. With the commerce came prosperity and that lured more people. Now, Corpus Christi was well on its way to becoming a full-fledged city.

The ship Fargo was looking for was out of France. It was called the *Relaise*. She was a four-master, a clipper out of Marseille. Two hundred and fifty feet long, she carried both passengers and cargo.

Finding her was easy. She was the only four-master at dock.

A sailor in a cap stopped Fargo at the bottom of the gangway.

"That is far enough, monsieur," he politely said in a heavy accent. "State your business, *s'il vous plaît*."

"I'm here to see the count," Fargo said. "He sent for me."

The sailor snapped straight and said, "Comte Louis Tristan of Valois?"

"That's his handle, if *comte* means count," Fargo said.

"Un moment," the sailor said. "I will be right back." And with that he hastened up the gangway.

Fargo hooked his thumbs in his gun belt. He didn't mind waiting. The count had sent him two hundred dollars as an advance against possible employment, so he'd hear the man out.

The sky was a vivid blue broken by a few puffy clouds. Gulls wheeled and squawked. The wind had momentarily stilled and the surface of the bay was a sheet of glass.

Fargo liked the sea but not nearly as much as the prairie and the mountains. Endless water wasn't the same as endless grass and neither could hold a candle to peaks that towered miles above the earth. He'd taken a voyage to Hawaii once, and that was enough of the ocean to last him a lifetime.

Feet pattered on the deck above and two figures appeared at the top of the gangway. Both took one look at him and put their hands over their mouths and giggled.

"Lord Almighty," Fargo breathed.

They were twins, near identical in every respect, with golden curls and eyes as blue as the sky. High cheekbones, delectable lips, and cantaloupes for bosoms added to their allure. Holding hands, they grinned coquettishly and sashayed down. Both were dressed in the height of European fashion, in sweeping dresses and hats that only females could love.

Fargo doffed his and said simply, "Ladies." If he had to guess, he'd peg their age at twenty or so.

They did more giggling and studied him openly from head to toe.

"Très beau, eh?" the twin on the right said.

"Magnifique," said the other.

The first one whispered in the ear of the second and both grinned like cats about to devour a canary.

"I'm Fargo," Fargo introduced himself. "I'm waiting on Count Louis. Could be you know him?"

"Oui, monsieur," said the twin on the left, giving a little curtsy.

"We know him quite well," said the other in English. "Better than most anyone except perhaps *notre mère.*"

"Our *maman,*" said the gorgeous vision on the left.

"Don't tell me," Fargo said.

"Oui," the twin on the right said.

"We are his daughters."

Fargo looked from one to the other and felt a stirring, down low. He hadn't heard what the job was yet but he'd already made up his mind.

He would take it.

No other series packs this much heat!

THE TRAILSMAN

#340: HANNIBAL RISING
#341: SIERRA SIX-GUNS
#342: ROCKY MOUNTAIN REVENGE
#343: TEXAS HELLIONS
#344: SIX-GUN GALLOWS
#345: SOUTH PASS SNAKE PIT
#346: ARKANSAS AMBUSH
#347: DAKOTA DEATH TRAP
#348: BACKWOODS BRAWL
#349: NEW MEXICO GUN-DOWN
#350: HIGH COUNTRY HORROR
#351: TERROR TOWN
352: TEXAS TANGLE
#353: BITTERROOT BULLETS
#354: NEVADA NIGHT RIDERS
#355: TEXAS GUNRUNNERS
#356: GRIZZLY FURY
#357: STAGECOACH SIDEWINDERS
#358: SIX-GUN VENDETTA
#359: PLATTE RIVER GAUNTLET
#360: TEXAS LEAD SLINGERS
#361: UTAH DEADLY DOUBLE
#362: RANGE WAR
#363: DEATH DEVIL
#364: ROCKY MOUNTAIN RUCKUS
#365: HIGH COUNTRY GREED

Follow the trail of Penguin's Action Westerns at
penguin.com/actionwesterns

National Bestselling Author

RALPH COMPTON

A WOLF IN THE FOLD
TRAIL TO COTTONWOOD FALLS
BLUFF CITY
THE BLOODY TRAIL
SHADOW OF THE GUN
DEATH OF A BAD MAN
RIDE THE HARD TRAIL
BLOOD ON THE GALLOWS
BULLET FOR A BAD MAN
THE CONVICT TRAIL
RAWHIDE FLAT
OUTLAW'S RECKONING
THE BORDER EMPIRE
THE MAN FROM NOWHERE
SIXGUNS AND DOUBLE EAGLES
BOUNTY HUNTER
FATAL JUSTICE
STRYKER'S REVENGE
DEATH OF A HANGMAN
NORTH TO THE SALT FORK
DEATH RIDES A CHESTNUT MARE
RUSTED TIN
THE BURNING RANGE
WHISKEY RIVER
THE LAST MANHUNT
THE AMARILLO TRAIL
SKELETON LODE
STRANGER FROM ABILENE
THE SHADOW OF A NOOSE
THE GHOST OF APACHE CREEK
RIDERS OF JUDGMENT
SLAUGHTER CANYON
DEAD MAN'S RANCH